MANDIE
AND THE
FOREIGN
SPIES

Mandie Mysteries

MANDIE
AND THE
FOREIGN SPIES

Lois Gladys Leppard

BETHANY HOUSE PUBLISHERS
MINNEAPOLIS, MINNESOTA 55438

Mandie and the Foreign Spies
Lois Gladys Leppard

Library of Congress Catalog Card Number 90-055639

ISBN 1-55661-147-1

Published by Bethany House Publishers
A Ministry of Bethany Fellowship, Inc.
6820 Auto Club Road, Minneapolis, Minnesota 55438

Printed in the United States of America

With love and appreciation to

BERGIN AND MINNIE CLAMPITT EDWARDS,

My Dearest North Carolina Cousins,

Who live in Mandie's neighborhood and

Who have helped me do local research.

Contents

"Then shalt thou call, and the Lord shall answer; thou shalt cry, and He shall say, Here I am."

Isaiah 58:9

Chapter 1 / Mysterious Greetings in London

"Sir, do you have a message for Amanda Shaw?" thirteen-year-old Mandie anxiously asked the clerk behind the counter of the telegraph office in London, England.

"I jolly well might have, miss." The man smiled back. "Are you Miss Amanda Shaw?"

"Yes, sir, I am." Mandie shifted her white kitten, Snowball, from one arm to the other as she rummaged in her drawstring bag for the piece of paper the messenger had brought to her on the ship.

Mandie's friend Celia reached for the kitten. "Let me hold him," she offered, taking Snowball.

Mrs. Taft, Mandie's grandmother, Senator Morton and the girls' friend, Jonathan, waited as Mandie finally pulled the paper out of her bag and handed it to the clerk.

"Your messenger brought this to me on the ship I just got off of," Mandie told the man as he read the paper. "You see, it says you have a message for me."

"That it does, miss," the man agreed. He turned to a row of pigeonholes behind him.

"It's probably from the United States," Mandie informed him as he checked each slot. "I don't know anyone here in England, so it must be from back home."

"Ah, here we are, miss," he said, withdrawing a small sheet of paper from the last opening. "Nope, it's not from the United States. Came from right here in London." He handed her the paper.

Mandie's bright blue eyes quickly scanned the message. She looked puzzled as she read it aloud, " 'Welcome to Europe. We are certain you will have an adventuresome time.' " She turned to her grandmother. "But it doesn't say who it's from."

Mrs. Taft read the few words on the paper and then asked the clerk, "Do you have the name of the person who sent this to my granddaughter?"

"No, madam, it isn't on the paper," the man replied.

"I know it isn't on the paper, but do you not have a record of people who send messages?" Mrs. Taft insisted.

"Begging your pardon, madam, but that message was here when I came to work tonight. I only log in the messages that come in while I am on duty," the man explained, smiling at Mandie.

"Is there no way to find out who sent it?" Mandie wanted to know.

The man glanced at an open book on the counter. "I fear not, miss," he replied. "Your name is not on the day's record here." He flipped the ledger around for Mandie to look at it.

Senator Morton stepped forward to look at the ledger. "Evidently there has been a slip-up somewhere," he said. "Perhaps we'll learn the sender's name later. Now I have a message to send, if you please."

Jonathan had been standing in the background and

now he stepped forward to the senator's side. "Senator Morton, sir, please emphasize in your message to my father that I have promised to stay with all of you until we go to Paris, where I will immediately contact my aunt and uncle," he begged.

"That way he won't come over here to get you before we've had time for you to show us around Europe," Mandie added.

Mandie and her girl friend, Celia Hamilton, were on a tour of Europe with Mandie's grandmother that summer of 1901. Jonathan Guyer had run away from his home in New York and the girls had found him stowing away on the ship.

Jonathan smiled at Mandie. "Yes, I hope he'll let me stay," he agreed.

"We'll see, son." The senator hastily scribbled a message on the pad on the counter, and Mandie turned her attention back to the message the clerk had given her.

"I just wish I knew who sent this," she said, staring at the words on the paper.

Celia smoothed Snowball's white fur as he clung to her. "I'd say it was from someone who knew you're always getting involved in all these adventures everywhere we go," she said.

"It sure sounds like Joe, but it couldn't have been him," Mandie said. "This message was sent from here in London, and Joe is back home in North Carolina."

"Who is Joe?" Jonathan asked.

"Oh, Joe is a friend I grew up with back home in Swain County. His father is Dr. Woodard, and he doctored my father until my father . . . died," Mandie haltingly added. Even now, over a year later, she still couldn't talk about her father's death. She loved him so much it was hard to make herself realize he was gone forever.

"Dr. Woodard travels around all over western North Carolina doctoring people everywhere," Celia said. "He's just about the only doctor in those mountains. And Joe is a *serious* friend of Mandie's, you might say."

"Celia!" Mandie gasped, her face burning red.

Jonathan shuffled his feet and dropped his gaze. "I see," he mumbled.

Senator Morton finished sending his message to Jonathan's father in New York and turned back to the group. "The answer will be sent to our hotel," he told Mrs. Taft. "Shall we go now?"

"Oh, yes. Let's do," Mrs. Taft agreed. "I'm beginning to feel like a good night's sleep."

Senator Morton told Jonathan, "I know your father will be glad to know that you are safe with us—that you haven't been kidnapped."

"He's going to be awfully angry with me for running away from home, though," Jonathan replied as they left the telegraph office.

The public carriage they had taken from the ship to the telegraph office had waited for them. Their luggage was piled high on top, and there was more to be delivered to the hotel.

"I do wish it were daylight," Mandie said, wistfully looking through the window of the carriage as it started on its way. Snowball curled up in her lap and went to sleep.

"We'll get up bright and early tomorrow to begin our sightseeing," Mrs. Taft promised.

As they rode along the cobblestone streets in the dark, Mandie saw shops and lots of people along the way. Then suddenly the street became lighter.

"Look!" Mandie pointed. "They have those newfangled lights up on posts along the street!" she cried.

"Amanda, those are gaslights," Mrs. Taft explained. "They've had those for many years."

"Oh," Mandie replied in disappointment.

Senator Morton smiled at her. "They do have those newfangled lights, as you call them, in the center of the city," he said. "We'll be seeing electric lights pretty soon now."

"Do you not have electric lights in North Carolina?" Jonathan asked.

"A few places have them," Mandie replied. "In Asheville, where Celia and I go to school, some of the stores have them, and our school is supposed to get them one day soon. But we don't have them at my house in Franklin."

"We have electric lights in New York," Jonathan told her.

"Look ahead, Amanda," Mrs. Taft said. "I believe I see electric lights up the street."

As the carriage rounded a curve, Mandie could see the street ahead through the open window. "I see them!" she said excitedly. "But you know, I don't think they are any brighter than the gaslights back there. I wonder why they don't just keep on using gaslights?"

Senator Morton laughed. "Every country tries to stay ahead of the others," he said. "They all want the latest invention as quickly as possible."

"Like the girls at school all trying to be the first to get the latest fashion in clothes," said Celia.

"I just don't see any sense in such stuff," Mandie replied, shifting the sleeping kitten in her lap.

"The Majestic Hotel, where we'll be staying, has electric lights," Jonathan told Mandie. "And the school I went to over here in London—well it's actually out in the country a ways—but it has electric lights, too. One day everyone everywhere will have electric lights."

"I suppose so," Mandie said with a sigh. "Talking about the Majestic Hotel, do you suppose that strange woman from the ship will be staying there?"

"Oh, I hope so," Celia said. "Then maybe we can find out who she is."

"Well, she'd better not follow us around like she did on the ship," Mandie remarked.

"If she is staying at the Majestic Hotel, she won't have a chance to follow us around because we are going to be busy every minute while we're here in London," Mrs. Taft said. "I want you girls to learn as much as you can about what you see. It will be so educational for y'all."

"Yes, ma'am," the two girls chimed.

Snowball got up and stretched, and the rattle of paper in Mandie's lap reminded her of the message she had received. She pulled the paper out from under the cat and smoothed it out.

"Do you suppose that strange woman could have sent me this message?" Mandie asked suddenly.

"Impossible," Jonathan told her. "She was on the ship with us, but the man said that message was sent by someone in London."

Mandie sighed. "I may never find out who it was."

The carriage pulled up in front of the doorway of the Majestic Hotel, and the driver jumped down and opened the door. Senator Morton assisted Mrs. Taft from the vehicle, and the young people quickly followed.

Mandie gasped as she gazed at the huge stone building in front of her. "My goodness!" she exclaimed.

"Looks like a castle!" Celia added.

"Oh, no, it's nothing like a castle," Jonathan said. "Wait till you see a real castle. It's not at all like this."

As the young people followed the adults into the lobby of the hotel, Mandie looked around in wonder. "I believe this is the fanciest building I've ever seen," she said.

Huge crystal chandeliers, electrically lighted, hung from the high ceiling. People mingled everywhere among the green plants about the marble-floored lobby. Rich red plush draperies covered the floor-length windows, and matching settees and chairs crowded the room. Conversation buzzed loudly with a hearty laugh here and there as friends greeted friends.

The girls stood there staring. Finally Mrs. Taft touched Mandie's shoulder and said, "Dear, you and Celia and Jonathan sit over there while the senator and I sign for our rooms."

"Yes, Grandmother," Mandie replied, not taking her eyes off the room around her as Mrs. Taft went with Senator Morton to the counter.

Mandie and her friends walked over to the settee Mrs. Taft had indicated, but suddenly three young dark-haired girls headed for the same seat. Not seeing the other girls, Mandie and Celia bumped into them as they all tried sitting down at the same time.

"Look out!" Jonathan tried to warn them, but he was too late. He had been in the hotel while he was a student in London and the finery was nothing new to him.

The five girls looked at each other and laughed.

Mandie straightened up and grasped Snowball tighter. He had almost escaped. "I'm sorry," she apologized to the girls.

Celia stood beside Mandie. "Me, too," she added.

The dark-haired girls also stood up. The smallest, a

pretty girl with dark eyes and dark skin, looked at Mandie and Celia curiously. "Why are you sorry?" she asked in an odd accent.

"I almost sat on you," Mandie said with a little laugh.

"There's enough room for us all," the tallest girl said, plopping down at the end of the long settee. "Sit down, please." She also spoke with an accent.

All five girls managed to squeeze onto the settee, but Jonathan was left standing.

As the girls laughed together, Jonathan suddenly stooped in front of the youngest girl, grasped her hand, kissed it, and said, *"Bonsoir, Mademoiselle, comment allez-vous?"*

The girl smiled and quickly replied, *"Comment vous appelez-vous?"*

Before Jonathan could answer, Mandie and Celia jumped up.

"Jonathan Lindall Guyer, the Third," Mandie said crossly, "you will not speak French around me ever again."

"Never!" Celia agreed.

"Didn't we get into enough trouble with your speaking French and pretending to be a foreigner on the ship?" Mandie reminded him.

"I'm sorry," Jonathan apologized mischievously. "I thought maybe these girls didn't understand English."

"Understand English?" The tallest girl gasped. "We happen to be very British and don't understand much French. I suppose you are all Americans."

At that moment a dignified-looking blonde woman and a handsome man with a light complexion came over to the three girls.

"Come, we are ready," the lady told them.

The three girls immediately became solemn. "Yes, Mother," they said in unison.

Rising from the settee, they followed the couple across the room. The youngest one looked back and secretly waved. Mandie and her friends watched them disappear into the crowd around the huge front doors.

"So, Jonathan," Mandie teased as they sat down on the settee again, "sooner or later their knowledge of French would have run out, and then you would have had to speak English."

"I'm really sorry, Mandie," Jonathan said. "I know French irritates you because I fooled you girls on the ship with it. However, when we go into France, you're going to have to put up with French because those people insist on speaking their own language!"

Mandie sat silently for a moment and then said, "Well, I just wasn't sure what you were saying to that girl."

Jonathan laughed loudly. "I only asked her how she was," he said, "and then she asked me what my name was."

"Jonathan, do you think you could teach us some French so we could talk to the people in France?" Celia asked.

Jonathan shrugged. "Maybe a few words, but you girls need to learn French in school," he replied. "It's convenient to know because most of the countries in Europe have people who speak or understand French."

"Did that girl tell you what her name was?" Mandie asked, petting Snowball's head as he tried to get down.

"No, you didn't give her time," Jonathan said, laughing.

"They all looked alike—except they were three different ages—didn't they?" Celia remarked.

Mandie laughed. "Now that's a jumbled sentence," she said. "In other words, they all looked like sisters."

"Yes." Celia nodded. "But, you know, they didn't look like the woman and man at all."

"No, they didn't," Jonathan agreed.

"But those people must have been the girls' parents because the girls all said 'Mother' together, remember?" Mandie told her friends.

"You're right," Jonathan said.

"I know, but they still didn't look like those people's daughters," Celia insisted.

"They're more than likely staying at this hotel, so we'll probably see them again," Mandie decided. "Next time I'll really look them over."

Senator Morton came through the crowd and stood beside the young people. "Come on, Mrs. Taft is ready to go upstairs," he said. "The bellhops have already taken care of our luggage. This way."

The senator led the way toward the counter and then headed down a corridor to the left. Mandie's grandmother was standing there waiting for them. Senator Morton stopped, and he and Mrs. Taft just stood there. Mandie looked around. She didn't see any stairs in this hallway. What were they waiting for?

Suddenly a hidden door opened in the wall in front of them and several people rushed through it from a sort of cage inside. Mandie watched in amazement.

Mrs. Taft stepped through the open doorway into the cage. "Come on, dears," she urged. "Hurry now."

Jonathan and Senator Morton immediately stepped aside, waiting for the girls to go ahead of them.

Mandie and Celia stood rooted to the spot.

"W-What is this?" Mandie exclaimed.

"It's a lift, Mandie," Jonathan tried to explain. "Or an elevator, as we would call it back home."

Mandie still hesitated. She remembered that her friend Joe had found an elevator at the White House when they were visiting Washington, D.C., but the elevator hadn't been working, so she had never been on one before.

Mrs. Taft waited for them inside the cage. "Come on, dears," she repeated.

Senator Morton urged, "Get in, young ladies, and we'll be on our way up to the fourth floor where our rooms are."

"Amanda!" Mrs. Taft was rapidly growing impatient.

Finally, Mandie and Celia slowly stepped inside next to her. When Jonathan and Senator Morton joined them, the door suddenly shut, and the girls held hands as the cage quickly ascended. Mandie's stomach felt funny, and she looked at Celia fearfully. Under her breath she declared that she would take the stairs up and down while they stayed at this hotel.

After a few seconds, Mandie noticed a man in uniform, who was evidently operating the contraption.

Snowball didn't seem to like the lift either. He tried to sink his claws into Mandie's shoulder as she held tightly to him with one hand. The elevator stopped with a sudden jerk and the door opened. When Mandie saw the hallway outside, she and Celia quickly rushed out. No one had to urge them this time.

"Whew!" the girls exclaimed.

Mandie bent her knees and lightly stomped her feet, trying to get the rubbery feeling out of her legs.

As Mrs. Taft and Senator Morton led the way down the corridor, Jonathan looked at the girls and laughed.

"Evidently you girls have never been in a lift before," he said.

Mandie told him about the elevator she and Joe had found at the White House. "But I have never seen the inside of such a contraption before," she said.

"Well, I've been on one," Celia told them, "but until today I've always refused to ride one again because it makes my stomach turn over."

"Mine, too," Mandie agreed. "Next time I'll take the stairs."

"You'll get used to it," Jonathan assured them.

Seeing Mrs. Taft beckoning to them from down the hallway, they rushed to catch up with her. She had stopped in front of an ornate door that was standing open. Senator Morton waited behind her.

"Come, girls," she told them. "This is our suite. Jonathan, you will share the one across the hall with Senator Morton."

Mandie and Celia stopped and waited for Mandie's grandmother to go inside. "Shall we breakfast at seven, Senator?" Mrs. Taft asked.

"Fine," Senator Morton agreed, opening the door to his suite.

Mandie silently groaned at the mention of being dressed for breakfast at seven the next morning. It was probably already past midnight.

After they all said good night, the girls closed the door to the suite and began looking around the huge room with brocade-covered mahogany furniture and plush carpets. A chandelier with electric lights gave a warm glow to the room.

"This is our parlor," Mrs. Taft explained. "Now I thought you girls should have the larger bedroom because you have twice as much luggage, so this is your room." She pushed open a door nearby to show an enormous bedroom with a canopied bed. "And my room is over there through the other door. Your bags are all here, so I suggest you girls quickly put on your nightclothes and get into bed. Seven o'clock will come around rather soon."

"Yes, ma'am," Mandie replied, looking around the spacious room. She spotted a box full of sand near the closed fireplace. "Look, they even gave us a box for Snowball."

"We requested it, dear," Mrs. Taft explained, turning to go to her room.

Mandie noticed a huge vase full of colorful flowers standing on a nearby table. "Aren't those beautiful?" she exclaimed. Then she saw something hanging on a ribbon from one of the blossoms. "There's a card here." She turned it over and read aloud, " 'Amanda Shaw, welcome to England.' " She looked at her grandmother. "My goodness, whoever put these flowers in here?" she asked.

Mrs. Taft hurried to inspect the card. "I have no idea, dear. There isn't even a signature on the card."

"All these crazy mysterious things keep happening!" Mandie exclaimed.

"Maybe the hotel put them here," Celia suggested.

"Perhaps they did," Mrs. Taft agreed. "Sometimes the better hotels put flowers in the suites. Anyway, let's all go to bed now. We can find out about the flowers in the morning."

Mrs. Taft turned to leave, but Mandie stopped her. "Is there a bathroom in this hotel?" she asked.

Her grandmother laughed. "I'm sorry, dear. I keep forgetting you are not familiar with such things. Try that door over there by the bureau."

Mandie quickly went to open it, and Celia followed, with Snowball right on their heels.

Mandie's eyes grew wide as she surveyed the inside of the bathroom. "My goodness, it's big enough to put the bed in there," she cried.

"It is as big as our room back at the school, isn't it?" Celia agreed.

"All right." Mrs. Taft laughed. "Good night now, dears. If you need me for anything I'll be right across the parlor in the other room."

Mandie untied her bonnet and took it off. Then she rushed to hug her grandmother. "Goodnight, Grandmother, and thank you for bringing me on this trip," she said.

Mrs. Taft kissed the top of Mandie's blonde head. "I should thank you for coming with me," she replied. "It's going to be an experience that I will treasure the rest of my days. When you are grown up, I'll remember your first journey to Europe. Now let's get some sleep, and I'll see y'all in the morning. Goodnight, Celia." Mrs. Taft lovingly reached to embrace Celia with her other arm.

Celia thanked Mrs. Taft for bringing her with them, and after another round of good nights, the girls went into their bedroom. Quickly taking off their travel-worn garments, they slipped into fresh cool nightgowns.

They were both so sleepy they could hardly hold their eyes open, but they were determined to discuss the mystery surrounding the message and the flowers. Poor Snowball was so exhausted, he curled up at his mistress's feet. Still the girls had plenty of room on the big bed. Mandie felt sure he wouldn't move all night.

After several minutes, Celia brought up the subject of

the strangers who had sat on the settee with them.

"I'd just like to know who they are," Mandie commented. "Maybe we could become friends with them. They said they were British. It would be nice to have friends in another country to write to, wouldn't it?"

"Yes, it would," Celia agreed. "But you know, Mandie, I believe there is some kind of mystery about those girls."

"That's funny. I was thinking the same thing," Mandie replied. "It might just be our imagination, but I think we ought to investigate."

"I agree," Celia replied sleepily, and the girls drifted off into dreamland.

Chapter 2 / Unsigned Warning

Mrs. Taft was right. Seven o'clock the next morning did come around pretty fast. Mandie and Celia were awakened by someone in their room opening the heavy draperies. Bright sunshine flooded the room. The girls sat up in bed in puzzlement, looking around.

"Oh, we're in London!" they said together.

"Yes, misses." A woman in uniform adjusted the last drapery and pointed to a tray she had set on the table nearby. "Your breakfast, misses. Is there anything else you would like?"

"No, thank you," Mandie replied. As she swung her feet off the side of the bed, Snowball tumbled off.

Mandie walked over to look at the tray full of steaming food. "Did you bring enough for my grandmother, too?" she asked the maid.

"I took Mrs. Taft her own tray before I came in here, miss," the woman explained. "Now, my name is Victoria. I will be your maid while you stay here."

"Victoria," Mandie repeated. "I suppose you were named for your Queen Victoria."

"Yes, miss," the stout woman answered.

"We read about her death in our newspapers back home in January," Celia remarked.

"Aye," Victoria replied. "But her son, Edward VII, is making a good king. Now if you wish nothing else at the moment, I will attend to the rest of your party across the hall. Good-day, misses." She quickly left the room.

"The rest of our party," Mandie mumbled as she stretched and yawned. "I suppose she's talking about Jonathan and Senator Morton."

Celia, still in her nightgown, sat down at the table and began filling a plate from the covered dishes of food.

"Come on, Mandie," she urged. "Let's hurry and eat. Time's a-wasting."

Mandie quickly joined her. "You're right. We don't want to waste a single minute in Europe. And I do hope Grandmother is up and getting ready for the day."

The girls heard a knock on the parlor door, and they listened as Mrs. Taft greeted Senator Morton.

"Good morning, Senator Morton."

"Good morning," came the senator's voice. "I believe I'm a little ahead of our planned schedule for this morning. But I've just received a reply to my message to Jonathan's father."

"That was fast," Mrs. Taft replied as the girls continued to listen.

"Yes, it was," Senator Morton said. "I hate to tell you this, but his father asks if we would immediately take Jonathan to his aunt and uncle in Paris. I know we had planned some time here in London first . . ."

"Oh." Mrs. Taft sounded a little disappointed.

By now the girls were watching from the parlor doorway. "We won't be seeing London!" Mandie whispered in a disappointed tone.

The senator continued. "Perhaps we could go on to Paris today, leave Jonathan there, then return to pick up our plans here."

"Of course," Mrs. Taft agreed. "I'll just check on the girls and hurry them up." As she started toward the girls' bedroom, Mandie and Celia scurried back to their breakfast.

Senator Morton called after her. "Shall we leave in— say, an hour?" he asked. "Will that give you time enough to prepare?"

"Plenty," Mrs. Taft agreed. "We'll only take whatever is necessary because we'll be coming back here."

Mandie leaned across the breakfast table and whispered to Celia, "That means Jonathan won't be able to travel with us around Europe."

"Maybe his aunt and uncle will give him permission to go with us," Celia whispered back.

"Girls," Mrs. Taft said from the bedroom doorway. "Please hurry and eat and get dressed. We have to go on to Paris today."

"Yes, ma'am," they replied.

"Pack only what you'll need for Paris," Mrs. Taft told them. "This hotel is to be our home base while we travel around. We'll be coming back here between visits to other places."

By the time the girls were ready, Senator Morton had engaged a private carriage to take them to the boat that would cross the English Channel to France.

As they road along the streets of London, the girls exclaimed over all the sights, and Jonathan explained about some of them.

Mandie shook her head. "The streets look so old and narrow," she noted. "And there are so many people everywhere you look."

"London is a huge city," Jonathan explained. "Sort of like New York, only I believe New York is larger."

"Look at all the people with carts on the streets," Celia said. "They're selling things, aren't they?"

"Right," Jonathan agreed. "You can buy all kinds of things from those sidewalk vendors. They even sell hot food. Some of it's pretty good."

"Oh, Jonathan, you know so much about things...," Mandie said, looking into the black eyes of the boy opposite her in the carriage. "I wish you could stay with us while we explore Europe."

Celia reached across and petted Snowball in Mandie's lap. "Do you think your aunt and uncle might let you travel with us?" she asked.

Jonathan smiled and said, "I'm sure going to find out."

"Did you ever keep a journal like we're doing when you traveled around different countries?" Mandie asked.

"No, that's girl stuff," Jonathan said. "Boys don't do things like that."

Mandie bristled. "Well, I'll have you know it was a man—Senator Morton—who suggested that Celia and I keep a journal of all our travels," she replied. "In fact, he's the one who gave us our notebooks just this morning."

Celia picked up the notebook in her lap. "I think it will be educational to write down as much as we can," she said.

"I'm just not the type to keep a journal," Jonathan told them. "You girls go ahead and write all you want, but not me. I'll even hold your kitten so you can start writing right now." He took Snowball from Mandie's lap.

"Thanks, Jonathan," Mandie said. She smoothly extracted a pencil from her drawstring bag.

Celia opened her book and took out her pencil, also. But the girls soon found that they couldn't look at the sights and write at the same time.

Mandie sighed in exasperation. "I have all these loose papers in my notebook, and they're all sliding out, so I think I'll just wait until we come to a stopping place somewhere to write." She closed the notebook and put her pencil back in her bag.

Jonathan smiled. "We're almost to the dock, anyway," he informed the girls.

They soon came to a stop, and the carriage driver helped them out. Senator Morton hurried to get the necessary tickets. A lot of people milled about them as they stood waiting for the senator to return. An old woman carrying a clothes basket walked by and bumped Mandie, causing Mandie to drop her journal. The wind caught the loose papers, scattering them everywhere. Mandie and her friends raced to gather them. The old woman didn't look back or speak but continued on her way through the crowd.

Mandie retrieved her notebook and began haphazardly stuffing the loose papers between the other sheets. "She could have at least said she was sorry," Mandie mumbled.

As Mrs. Taft watched, she remarked, "Maybe she didn't know she ran into you, dear."

"I'm sure she did, Grandmother. That was a strong bump she gave me," Mandie said, standing up with her journal in one hand and holding Snowball with the other.

"Your papers are in a mess," Celia told her.

"I'll straighten them out when we sit down somewhere," Mandie replied.

Senator Morton rejoined them with the tickets, and

they all moved ahead in the line to the waiting boat. He had also engaged a man to carry their luggage.

"Just think!" Mandie exclaimed. "We've already been in one country, and now we're going into another one, all in the same day."

"Move along, girls," Mrs. Taft urged as she preceded the young people onto the boat. "Find seats now. We'll soon be on our way."

"Over here," Jonathan suggested, turning toward the long bench around the railing.

"It might be pretty windy out here," Mrs. Taft warned them. "The senator and I will sit inside." She followed Senator Morton through the doorway.

As the young people sat down, they surveyed the other passengers. The boat was not crowded, and most of the passengers were well dressed.

"They must all be sightseers like us," Mandie remarked.

"There's not much reason to travel from one country to the other unless you're sightseeing nowadays," Jonathan agreed.

"Mandie, give me Snowball so you can straighten out your notebook while we're sitting," said Celia, reaching out to take the white kitten.

"It is a mess," Mandie agreed. She opened the cover and started to sort out the loose papers. There was one dirty crumpled piece and she paused to inspect it. "Oh, goodness, this really got beat up in the shuffle. Wait a minute. This isn't mine. How did it get in my journal? Look." She held the paper out for her friends to see.

"Another mystery!" Celia cried.

Jonathan took the paper and began reading aloud. "It says, 'Be careful in Paris.'" He handed the paper back to Mandie. "Now what do you suppose that means?"

Mandie slapped her notebook shut. "Why do these things keep happening?" she asked angrily.

Jonathan eyed her curiously. "Where have you had your journal?" he asked. "Did someone else pick it up, maybe, and put that paper in it?"

"No," Mandie replied. "Senator Morton just gave us these journals this morning, and I put all those brochures and things in it because they wouldn't fit in my bag." She held up her small drawstring bag.

"You probably picked it up by mistake when you dropped the notebook," Celia said, holding the squirming kitten tighter as the boat began to move.

"I suppose I must have," Mandie agreed. "That's the only possible explanation." She turned the paper over and over to inspect it, then finally opened the cover of her notebook and tucked it inside.

"Are you going to keep that dirty paper?" Celia asked.

Mandie paused and looked around. "What else can I do with it? I can't just throw it on the floor."

"There will be a can for refuse nearby when we dock," Jonathan suggested. "You can get rid of it then."

But when the boat finally docked, the young people became excited about going ashore and forgot about the piece of paper.

Mrs. Taft and Senator Morton were already outside in line, waiting to leave the boat, and the young people hurried through the crowd to join them.

Suddenly Mandie stopped, causing her friends to collide with her. "Look!" she cried, pointing across the deck through the crowd.

"What?" Celia asked with a puzzled gaze.

"Something wrong?" Jonathan asked, looking in the direction she pointed.

"She's gone now," Mandie moaned. "Didn't you see her? I'm sure it was that strange woman from the ship. I know it was!"

"Where?" Celia asked, "Where was she?"

"Over there, that way." Mandie pointed again. "She probably saw me and hid behind somebody."

"Amanda!" Mrs. Taft called from the exit. "Hurry up."

"Yes, ma'am," Mandie replied. She and her friends hurried to catch up.

"Are you positive that was the woman from the ship?" Jonathan asked. "The one who seemed to be following you girls around everywhere?"

"I'm sure it was," Mandie confirmed, taking Snowball from Celia.

"Do you suppose she's still following us, or just happens to be going where we're going?" Celia asked.

"She may happen to be going where we're going—on *purpose*," Mandie said.

"You're probably right," Celia agreed.

As they stepped onto land, Mandie looked ahead at the dirty harbor. "Is *this* Paris?" she asked.

"Goodness, no," Jonathan quickly replied. "This is the dock for Le Havre. Paris is inland, not on the coast. We'll have to get another carriage to go on to Paris."

Mrs. Taft turned to explain, "We will eat something when we get into town. It's going to be late before we arrive in Paris."

"Thank goodness! We're going to eat," Jonathan exclaimed, patting his stomach.

Mandie kept looking back as the young people moved toward the waiting carriage, "I was hoping to see that woman. She has to get off the boat or turn around and go back to England," Mandie explained to her friends.

"Do you suppose she'll go on to Paris?" Celia wondered aloud as they hurried along.

"Paris is a big city," Jonathan remarked. "She'll have trouble keeping up with us if she's headed there."

The senator and Mrs. Taft were waiting at the carriage. "Let's go," Mrs. Taft directed, climbing inside.

While Senator Morton waited, the girls and Jonathan found their seats, and then he joined them.

Mandie looked around as the driver got the carriage rolling. "Where is our luggage?"

"We sent it ahead to the hotel in Paris, dear," Mrs. Taft explained.

"I'm glad we are staying in a hotel in Paris," Mandie replied.

"Yes, dear, it would be too far to go and come in one day. Besides, it may take time to find Jonathan's relatives," Mrs. Taft reminded them. "We will go into Le Havre in this carriage, have a meal, get refreshed and then go on to Paris."

Mandie sighed, cuddling Snowball in her arms. "It sure is complicated to get around Europe," she sighed. "Even Snowball is plumb tuckered out."

"Remember, Mandie," Jonathan said, "we are going from one country to another here. In the United States it would be the same as going from state to state because the countries here are so much smaller than our country."

"You're right." Mandie nodded. "Imagine if all our states were different countries."

"I'm glad they aren't," Celia remarked. "We'd have to learn all kinds of languages to travel at home!"

The carriage stopped, and Mandie and her friends looked outside at a gray stone building. A sign hanging on a pole read: The Monkey's Tail Inn.

Giggles overtook them when they read it. Mandie finally regained her composure enough to say, "We're in France, but the sign is in English."

Jonathan laughed. "Probably an Englishman owns it."

Other vehicles were drawn up around the building, and inside the place was crowded. Every seat and table was taken.

A tall, thin man in a white apron came forward to greet them. He smiled under his black mustache and bowed slightly. "We are pleased to have you partake of our food," he said. "Please follow me. We have a quiet room this way."

The young people almost broke into giggles again, but a stern look from Mrs. Taft put a stop to that.

The man led them through a side door, down a long hallway, and into a pleasant dining room where a few diners were seated. He showed them to a long table with dishes and silverware already placed on it.

"We have a delicious roast today," the man said as he helped Mrs. Taft get seated. "We have sauerkraut and nice field peas."

"We'll be glad to be served whatever you have," Mrs. Taft told him.

"And we would be appreciative if you could hurry the food," Senator Morton told the man. "You see, we're on our way to Paris."

"*Oui, monsieur,*" the man replied. "Yes, sir. You will have your food soon." He left the room.

The young people watched the other people in the

room. Snowball curled up contentedly in Mandie's lap.

"Mandie, aren't those the girls we saw at the hotel in London?" Celia asked, slightly nodding her head toward a table at the other end of the long room.

Mandie looked, but the girls had their backs toward her, so she couldn't be sure. "Might be," she said, continuing to watch them.

At that moment, a heavy-set woman in a white apron brought food to the table where the three dark-haired girls sat with other people. As the woman moved to set the dishes on the table, one of the girls turned to look at her, and Mandie got a glimpse of the girl's face.

"Yes, those *are* the girls," Mandie said in a loud whisper.

"Well, well. I wonder where they are going," Celia remarked.

"Everybody seems to be going our way today," Jonathan said. "Maybe we'll meet up with the girls on our way out."

"And talk French?" Mandie shook her head. "Oh no, Jonathan Lindall Guyer, the Third."

"All right, all right," Jonathan replied. "I just thought we might ask them where they're going."

Mrs. Taft and Senator Morton were engrossed in their own conversation when the waiter returned with a large tray heaped with steaming dishes.

He handed Mandie a small empty bowl and said, "For the kitty-cat." Mandie smiled and thanked him.

Mandie filled the bowl with food and gave it to Snowball under the table.

"Good. The food is here. Thank you for the quick service," Mrs. Taft said.

Senator Morton led in prayer and everyone began to eagerly enjoy the meal.

Halfway through the meal Mandie noticed a commotion across the room. Snowball had scampered to the table where the three girls sat.

In her haste to get up, Mandie almost knocked her chair over. Rushing across the room, she snatched up her cat and stammered an apology.

The girls didn't say a word, but the woman with them said haughtily, "We accept your apologies. Now be gone!"

Mandie's face turned red with anger, and she quickly hurried back to her own table and sat down, holding on to Snowball as tightly as possible.

Everyone was waiting to hear what had happened.

Mandie took a deep breath after explaining that she had apologized. "Those are the same three girls from the hotel, and that woman with them is rude," she said.

Her grandmother comforted her. "Don't worry, dear. You apologized. That's all you could do. We'll be on our way shortly and will probably never see the people again."

"I don't know about that," Mandie said under her breath.

Chapter 3 / Paris at Last

The journey to Paris was exciting to Mandie and Celia as they watched the scenery go by. They traveled through small villages and beautiful countryside, discussing it all during rest stops at small country inns. Around five o'clock the driver stopped the carriage in front of a small but expensive-looking hotel. It was time for afternoon tea.

Mrs. Taft rose to leave the vehicle. "We only have about fifteen minutes here, so hurry and freshen up."

Senator Morton assisted Mrs. Taft down the steps of the carriage, then said to Mandie and the others, "I've stopped here before. I believe the water closets are inside."

Mandie and Celia looked puzzled.

Celia turned to Jonathan. "Water in a closet?"

"In Europe they call toilets water closets," he explained matter-of-factly.

"Oh," the girls said, dropping their gaze.

The senator and Mrs. Taft had already disappeared inside. "Come on," Jonathan urged. "I'm sure you'll find mirrors in the water closet. They always have the latest thing here in France."

The three hurried through the big arched doorway. Mrs. Taft and Senator Morton were seated at a small table for refreshments.

Jonathan led the girls through the huge room to a door labeled *le lavabo*. "There you are," he announced. He turned away and went to sit with the adults.

Mandie and Celia paused to read the French words on the door, then went inside. One whole wall of the room was covered with floor-length mirrors.

Mandie gasped at her reflection. "No wonder Jonathan told us they had mirrors in here." Setting her kitten on the floor, she straightened her skirt and tucked loose strands of her blonde hair under her bonnet.

Celia bent to wash her hands at the small, low lavatory. "We *do* look travel-worn, don't we?" She turned on the faucet, and jumped back suddenly as the water gushed out with a loud roar. Both girls were overcome again with giggles.

"They also have rumbling water here!" Mandie exclaimed. When Celia finished, Mandie washed and then found an empty tin on a shelf. She filled it with water and set it on the floor for Snowball. He eagerly lapped up the cool liquid.

"I think we'd better get something to drink too," Celia remarked.

"Yes, and we'd better hurry," Mandie added, "Grandmother will wonder what is keeping us." She picked up Snowball.

When they reached the table, small glasses of a dark purple drink were already at their places.

Mandie picked up her glass to smell it. "What is it?" she asked.

"It's grape juice, dear," Mrs. Taft answered. "I keep

forgetting that you haven't been to Europe before. You see, we're in grape country."

"They grow grapes here?" Mandie asked, sipping the juice. "It's delicious."

Celia tasted the drink. "I've had grapes before, but not the juice. It tastes almost as good as grapes do."

Jonathan smiled. "I do hope I will be permitted to stay with all of you while you're in Europe. It would be such fun to show you around," he told the girls.

"I hope you can, too," Mandie replied as Celia added, "I do, too."

Once in the carriage again, they settled down for the rest of the trip to Paris. As they drove off, Mandie noticed another carriage pull in and stop in front of the hotel. Glancing back, she saw the same three dark-haired girls emerge from the vehicle, along with the man and woman who accompanied them everywhere.

Mandie sighed. "There they are again."

"I just wish we could turn around and follow them," Celia commented.

"Now that would be fun," Jonathan added. "Maybe they'll catch up and pass us somewhere."

———

But they didn't see the girls again that day. The sun gradually slipped down in the west and dimmed the day into darkness. All they could see was the faint lamplight in the cottages they passed.

Mandie looked into the darkness. "Oh, shucks! I wish we could have gotten to Paris before dark."

"You'll have all day tomorrow to see it, dear," Mrs. Taft told her. "We plan to find Jonathan's aunt and uncle in the morning, and then spend the rest of the day sight-seeing."

"And don't forget how many countries we're going to visit," Senator Morton reminded them. "We'll be in Switzerland, Italy, Germany, the Netherlands, Belgium, Scotland, Wales and Ireland, if our plans work out."

"I'm just breathless with excitement!" Celia enthused.

"We'll really have something to tell those girls back at school!" Mandie exclaimed. Then a thought crossed her mind about school. "Celia! Do you know what's going to happen?"

"No. What?" Celia asked.

"Miss Prudence will probably ask us write a report on our journey!" Mandie groaned.

"But that won't be hard to do if you girls keep up with your journals," Jonathan said.

"Yes, I'm going to start a habit of writing in my journal the last thing every night before I go to bed," Mandie decided. "That way I'll be able to cover the whole day's activities." She shifted Snowball onto the seat next to her, and he curled up in a ball to continue his nap.

"Then all we'll have to do is copy out of our journals for the report," Celia enthused.

Suddenly the whole sky seemed to light up before them. Mandie and Celia leaned on the open window to see ahead.

"Is something on fire?" Mandie asked.

Jonathan stood and bent over the girls' heads to see out.

"No," he said. "It's *la ville de la lumière*."

"The what?" Mandie asked, looking at him.

"The city of lights," he explained. "Paris has so many

electric lights the French call it *la ville de la lumière*."

"That glow is from electric lights? There must be a million of them!" Mandie exclaimed. She turned back to watch the road ahead.

Mrs. Taft paused in her conversation with Senator Morton. "There just may be a million of them, dear," she told her granddaughter. "They have electric lights in most of the theatres, stores, the railway station, and even on the national monuments—not to mention the street lights."

As they approached the city, Mandie and Celia eagerly clung to the open window, in order not to miss a thing.

"A river!" Celia exclaimed as they neared water.

The carriage turned and they drove alongside it. "That's the River Seine," Jonathan told them.

The lights illuminated the crowds of people, the many, many shops, sidewalk cafes, parks, and impressive buildings. The girls were so excited they couldn't think of anything else to say. They could only breathe "oh" and "ah" as the city unfolded before them.

Mrs. Taft, sitting on the opposite side of the carriage, drew their attention to the view from her window. "Look, girls, what do you suppose that tall structure is over there?" she asked with a teasing smile.

The girls jumped to the other side of the carriage and gazed outside.

"The Eiffel Tower!" Mandie and Celia exclaimed together. They squeezed each other's hand. "Wow!" Mandie added. "It's bigger than I thought it would be."

"Look at all the lights on it!" Celia cried.

"Do you girls know the story of the Tower?" Senator Morton asked.

The girls pulled their heads back inside. "Not really,"

Mandie said. "I do know it's the tallest metal structure in the world."

Celia nodded. "And it was built for France's 1889 World's Fair," she said. "Mandie and I are one year older than it is."

"You are both correct," the senator agreed. "It was designed by the same man who engineered the structural framework of our Statue of Liberty. You know, of course, that the statue was given to us by France. Alexandre Gustave Eiffel is still living, by the way. He's about sixty-eight years old, I believe."

Jonathan's black eyes sparkled. "You can see the Eiffel Tower from all over Paris," he added. "And they say there are so many visitors from other countries that you can hear almost every language in the world spoken there."

"Thank goodness we're almost to our hotel," Mrs. Taft said, changing the subject. "We seem to be moving at a snail's pace."

Snowball stretched and yawned, and then began his usual ritual of washing himself after a nap.

Mandie patted her kitten's head. "We'll soon be out of this bumpy, pokey carriage, Snowball," she said. "Where are we staying, Grandmother?"

"The Hotel Rochambeau," Mrs. Taft replied. "It's in the center of practically everything we want to see. And it's a clean, well-maintained place."

The carriage began to move a little faster. "Are we going to the hotel now for the night?" Mandie asked. "Are we not going to look around first?"

"It's late, Amanda," Mrs. Taft said. "You don't realize it because the French people eat late in the evening and stay up all hours of the night. And we're used to doing things earlier."

Mandie peered out the window of the carriage again. "But it's still light, Grandmother," she said.

"The electric lights make it seem that way. Once you leave the main streets it is dark."

"But we're on vacation," Mandie persisted. "Couldn't we take a little walk after we check into the hotel? Please?"

Mrs. Taft glanced at the senator. "We older people like to relax awhile in the evening before we retire," she said.

"Oh," said Senator Morton, "I believe my legs could use a good stretching after all this riding." He winked at Mandie. "If you don't mind, I'd be happy to escort these youngsters around the block."

The three looked at each other, waiting for Mrs. Taft's reply.

"Well now, Senator, I didn't want to impose on you, but if you feel up to a turn around the square, then we'll all go," Mrs. Taft said, smiling.

"Thanks," Mandie said excitedly, turning back to the window.

Approaching the hotel, they fell into line with several other vehicles waiting to get to the front door. People and baggage were being discharged ahead of them, and there were loud conversations all around them on the streets.

"Oh, shucks, I can't understand a thing anyone is saying," Mandie remarked.

The others laughed.

"Of course not," Jonathan told her. "They're speaking French. You've just got to learn the language, Mandie."

Ignoring Jonathan's comment, Mandie continued to listen to the buzz of conversation outside. Suddenly she said, "I hear someone speaking English!"

"Where?" Celia asked.

"Over there," Mandie said, pointing out the window. "No, that way I think." She shook her head. "Now I don't hear it at all."

"Was it British-style English or American English?" Celia asked.

"I suppose it was British, probably someone who came over from London like we did," Mandie said.

"Like those people?" Jonathan asked, quickly drawing the girls' attention to the carriage second in line in front of them.

Mandie and Celia gasped.

"It's the three girls!" Mandie exclaimed. "Now how did they get ahead of us?"

"They could have passed us without our noticing them in all that crazy traffic," Celia remarked.

The three dark-haired girls left the carriage and disappeared inside the doorway of the hotel. The couple with them seemed to give instructions to the carriage driver and then followed the girls inside. When the carriage pulled away, the next one took its place in front of the hotel.

"We're next," Celia said.

"Maybe we can still catch up with those people." Mandie commented.

Mrs. Taft spoke up. "Amanda," she began in a warning tone, "judging from the way that woman spoke to you in the inn, I would say that those people are not very well bred. Therefore, I forbid you to have any communication with them. Do you understand?"

Mandie looked at her grandmother in surprise. "Yes, ma'am," she answered. "But I am curious as to who they really are and why we keep seeing them."

"That can be easily explained. They must be traveling,

as we are, and happen to be going our way at the same time," Mrs. Taft said. "Let's just forget about those people and enjoy our visit here."

"Yes, Grandmother," Mandie said. "I can't wait to get outside."

Even though there had been a line to get into the hotel, the lobby was not crowded. Mandie and Celia and Jonathan waited nearby while the adults checked in at the desk.

Mandie watched the man behind the counter bow to her grandmother as he took her hand and kissed it. Then he summoned a bellhop. Mrs. Taft and Senator Morton beckoned for the young people to follow as they headed down the long marble-floored corridor.

"Celia," Mandie whispered, "my grandmother didn't sign in, and neither did the senator! Do you think—"

"That the man knew your grandmother?" Celia asked.

Jonathan added, "Or that your grandmother owns the place, like the ship we were on?"

"Both," Mandie replied.

As they neared the elevators, Celia moaned. "Oh, Mandie, I don't want to ride in one of those lifts again. Let's find the stairway, quick!"

They stopped to look around, and then they saw the bellhop opening a door down the long hallway and motioning for Mrs. Taft to enter.

"Never mind," Mandie said. "It looks like we're staying on this floor."

When they caught up with the adults, they found that Mandie was right. Mrs. Taft ushered them into a suite similar to the one they had occupied in London, and the senator and Jonathan were shown into the suite next door to them.

The girls looked curiously around the bedroom before freshening up. "No messages, no flowers. Good!" Mandie said.

"Right!" Celia agreed.

Soon everyone was ready for a walk, and Mandie couldn't decide whether to take Snowball with her or leave him in their suite. Her grandmother made the decision for her. "I think you'd better take him with you, dear," she said. "The maid might come in and let him out accidentally. We don't want to have to look all over Paris for a lost kitten."

So the three agreed to take turns holding him as they followed Mrs. Taft and the senator through the hotel lobby and outside to the wide sidewalk. People were milling about everywhere, in no particular hurry it seemed. There was loud talking and laughing as if it were the middle of the day.

As they left the vicinity of the hotel, Mandie saw vendors at the street curbs, selling everything imaginable. "Whew!" she sighed. "This town makes me plumb dizzy. I've never seen so many people."

Jonathan was holding Snowball when everyone heard a loud roar and a horn blowing nearby. Mrs. Taft and Senator Morton stopped suddenly, and the young people almost bumped into them as a strange machine came chugging past. Jonathan had to struggle to keep Snowball from escaping.

Mandie's blue eyes grew wide in wonder as she stared at the self-propelled vehicle which had come to a stop in the street ahead. "What is *that*?" she exclaimed.

Jonathan laughed. "Why that's a motor car. Haven't you ever seen one?"

"No!" Mandie and Celia squeaked.

"Well, let's go take a look," the senator suggested.

Mandie's legs were trembling as she forced them to move forward. *A motor car!* She had heard vaguely of such a thing but had never expected to see one.

Celia clung to Mandie's hand, and Jonathan held tightly to the squirming kitten. As they approached the vehicle, Mandie asked Jonathan, "Why is there no horse to pull it?"

"It has a motor inside and you put gasoline, or petrol as they call it in England, in the motor and that makes it go," Jonathan explained. "My father is planning to buy a motor car in New York."

"They probably cost a fortune," Mandie remarked.

"But Jonathan's father has a lot more than a fortune, remember?" Celia reminded her.

When they got close enough to see the people in the motor car, Mandie took a deep breath. "Oh, no! It's those three girls and that man and woman with them."

"You're right," Jonathan agreed.

At that moment the motor car made a terrible screeching noise, and the man drove off. Vendors nearby applauded enthusiastically.

"I can't believe it was those people again...." Mandie said to her grandmother.

"Well, at least you got to see a real motor car," Mrs. Taft said.

Snowball chose that moment to escape from Jonathan. He jumped down to the cobblestoned sidewalk and immediately leaped on top of one of the vendor's carts nearby. The man caught the kitten and laughed good-naturedly.

Mandie rushed after him. "Oh, I'm sorry," she said to the vendor, taking Snowball from him. The man didn't seem to understand her and said something in French.

Mrs. Taft and Jonathan began speaking to the man at the same time in French.

"Excuse me," Jonathan apologized to Mrs. Taft.

"That's all right. You go ahead and talk to the man," Mrs. Taft said.

Jonathan explained in French that he was the one responsible for letting the kitten escape. The man smiled and picked up a bright red braided rope with some loops on the end of it and offered it to Mandie, speaking rapidly in his native language.

Mandie looked at Jonathan and took the rope somewhat hesitantly. "What is this? What am I supposed to do with it?" she asked.

"I'll show you," Jonathan said. Taking the kitten from her and securing him tightly with one hand, he slipped the red rope loops around the kitten's head and shoulders and pulled up on it. Then he handed the long rope to Mandie. "Put him down now and hold on to this leash. He can't get away from you anymore," he explained.

Mandie looked doubtfully at Snowball and set him down. The kitten rolled over and over attempting to get out of the harness.

"It won't work," Mandie said as the kitten became tangled up in the rope. "I tried using a leash with him before, and he didn't like it."

"I think it will work, Amanda," Mrs. Taft said. "You just have to be patient and teach him to obey you. When he finds out you're not going to take it off, he'll probably quit trying to get out of it."

Mandie stooped down and shook her finger at the kitten. "Snowball! Stop that! Get up!" she demanded.

Snowball quit wiggling to gaze at his mistress. After

a moment he stood up and looked at Mandie and meowed pitifully.

"It's for your own good, Snowball," Mandie told him. "If we lost you in this big town, I'd probably never find you again."

Snowball meowed again.

"See if you can get him to walk along with you," Celia suggested.

Mrs. Taft took money from her bag and was trying to pay the vendor, but he waved her away. He laughed as Mandie gently pulled on the leash, and Snowball tried his best to follow her without stumbling.

"The French think of everything, don't they?" Jonathan remarked.

"I'm not sure Snowball is going to cooperate with this," Mandie said.

But the kitten did behave all the way back to the hotel. Then when Mandie released him in their suite, he cut capers all over the bedroom. The girls burst into giggles.

Suddenly Mandie stopped giggling. "Celia! Look!" she pointed to her journal. Its loose papers were strewn all over the rug on the far side of the big bed.

The girls quickly gathered everything up. Mandie tried to straighten out the loose papers and tuck them back inside the notebook.

"Is everything all right?" Celia asked.

"I think so," Mandie said, closing the notebook and placing it on the nearby table. "It looks like it's all there anyway."

"Good," Celia said. "Who do you think was in here?"

"I don't know," Mandie said. Suddenly she reached for the notebook again and flipped through it. "Wait! I thought everything was here, but there *is* one thing missing!"

"What's that?" cried Celia.

"That dirty scrap of paper with the message that said 'Be careful in Paris.' "

"Maybe it's under the bed," Celia offered. She quickly stooped to look under the big high bed. Mandie joined her.

Then they searched all over the room but couldn't find it.

Mandie sat on the floor as Snowball romped around her. "Now I'm sure that somebody slipped that note into my papers on purpose in London," she said. "They must have done it when I dropped my notebook. And now they've taken it back. I wonder what's going on."

"It's scary, Mandie," Celia said seriously.

"It's aggravating!" Mandie said emphatically as she rose. "Guess we'd better get ready for bed before Grandmother checks on us." She picked up her nightgown and paused thoughtfully. "I wish Joe could have come with us."

"I do, too," Celia agreed. "He always knows what to do about things."

After the girls had dressed for bed, Celia picked up her notebook from the table. "Mandie, don't you think we'd better write something in our journals for the day?"

"You're right, Celia," Mandie replied, "I almost forgot. I'll talk to Jonathan in the morning about the missing note. Maybe he'll have some ideas." Plopping down on the bed, she began writing about the day's events while Celia sat across the room doing the same in her journal.

As Mandie wrote, her hand slowed, and her thoughts turned toward home. She wondered what her mother and stepfather (who was also her uncle) were doing, and how the new baby was. And where was her dear old Cherokee friend, Uncle Ned? She missed him already. He always seemed to show up when she needed him. And her life-long friend Joe, who was determined that they were going to marry when they grew up. What was he doing, she wondered.

I'm not going to get homesick, she told herself. *I'm going to enjoy my visit here in Europe—in spite of all the mysterious goings-on.* First, it was the strange woman on the ship who followed them everywhere, and still turned up now and then, and then the unsigned message in London, and the unaccounted-for flowers in her hotel room. And the three dark-haired sisters, who also kept turning up, and now the mystery of the missing note. Could all these things be connected to one person? What did it all mean?

Mandie was determined to find out.

Chapter 4 / Missing Relatives

Snowball woke Mandie the next morning. Although he usually slept on the foot of her bed without stirring, this morning he had crawled up on her pillow and was purring loudly in her ear.

Mandie opened her sleepy eyes. "Snowball, what's the matter with you?" she mumbled.

The white kitten jumped down to the floor.

Confused, Mandie sat up in the big bed. The sun peeked through a fold in the drapery that was not closed properly. Then she remembered where she was. Celia was already awake beside her.

Celia laughed. "He woke me up too," she said.

Mandie reached over to the table for her watch, which she wore on a chain around her neck. "Snowball must be hungry," she said, flipping the cover on her watch face to see the time. "Celia, it's just ten minutes to six." Looking at the opening in the drapery, she added, "And I believe the sun is already up."

"Do you know if we'll have a maid here like we did in London to open the curtains and bring us our breakfast?" Celia asked.

"I don't know, but I'll beat her to the curtains," Mandie said, rushing across the room. As she pulled back the heavy draperies, the sunlight streamed through, and she turned to go back to the bed.

"Mandie! There are people out there! They can see in!" Celia gasped, quickly sliding under the sheet.

Mandie returned to the window to see what was going on outside. "Celia, they're sitting at tables out there and eating, I think," Mandie told her as she stood back from the window. "My grandmother probably didn't think about anything like this when she took these rooms on the ground floor." She kept watching the people outside.

"Mandie, please close the curtains so we can get dressed," Celia begged, still under the sheet.

Mandie reached for the drapery pull, and then stopped. "Celia, Jonathan is out there!" she exclaimed. "And you won't believe who else! Those three girls we've been seeing everywhere!"

Celia jumped out of bed and crept to Mandie's side to view the scene.

"Where are the man and woman that are usually with them?" Celia asked.

"I don't know," Mandie answered. "But what on earth are they doing out there so early in the morning?"

"They're eating," Celia shrugged.

"I know, but why so early?" Mandie replied, still curiously watching the foursome. "They sure are doing a lot of talking about something."

"Mandie, look at these windows," Celia said, "I believe they open up like doors. See, they go all the way down to the floor. We could get dressed and go outside."

"This early?" Mandie replied. "I don't think my grandmother would approve of that. Well, Jonathan finally got a chance to talk French with those girls!" She yanked the draperies shut, rushed over to the bathroom door and said, "I'm going to get dressed."

Celia plopped down on the side of the bed. "Why, Mandie, I do believe you're jealous," she teased.

Mandie whirled around. "No, I'm not! It's just that—oh, I'm going to get dressed." She went into the bathroom and closed the door.

Someone tapped softly on the parlor door, and Celia went to answer it.

A tall, thin woman in a neat uniform rolled a teacart into the parlor as she said, "*Bonjour*. I bring food." Then she went to open the parlor draperies. Mandie stepped to the bedroom door and looked out, expecting to see Jonathan and the girls. There was nothing there but a flower garden. Obviously the parlor windows opened onto a different side of the hotel.

The woman turned and spoke rapidly in French to Celia, gesturing with her hands, and walked to the door.

"Thank you," Celia said.

The woman smiled and waved as she left the room.

Celia turned back into the bedroom. "Mandie!" she said, surprised to see her friend was already dressed. "The maid brought us some food." She motioned toward the parlor.

"Good," Mandie replied. "I'm hungry. Are you going to dress before we eat?"

Celia nodded and went to peek behind the curtain that opened to the outdoor eating area. "Jonathan is gone," she said to Mandie.

Mandie shrugged and pursed her lips, pretending she wasn't interested.

By the time Celia was dressed and they'd begun eating, Mrs. Taft had joined them to discuss their schedule for the day. "We'll be leaving as soon as the senator is ready," she said, helping herself to coffee. "We'll drop Jonathan off at his aunt's house and then—how would you girls like to go up the Eiffel Tower?"

Mandie asked excitedly, "You mean it's possible to go up the tower?"

"Well, we'll go part of the way, just so you girls can enjoy the view," Mrs. Taft replied. "And then maybe we'll go to the Louvre and look at some art work."

"Could we eat at one of those little places where you sit at a table on the sidewalk?" Mandie asked.

"Of course, dear," Mrs. Taft replied. "You girls may choose what you'd like to do. After all, this trip to Europe is especially for y'all." She patted both girls' hands.

"Thank you, Grandmother." Mandie's smile lit up her blue eyes.

"I'm so grateful to you for bringing me along, Mrs. Taft," Celia told her.

"Well, after all, your mother and Amanda's mother are childhood friends," Mrs. Taft said. "I'm glad you could come."

There was a knock on the parlor door and Mandie rose. "I'll see who it is, Grandmother," she offered.

Senator Morton and Jonathan greeted her at the door, ready for the day. She invited them in, and they were all soon on their way.

Neither of the girls had much to say to Jonathan as they walked down the long hallway toward the hotel lobby.

Leading the way to the front desk, Senator Morton reminded them that they must all exchange some American money for French currency.

Mrs. Taft, who was in charge of the money for Mandie

and Celia, gave the clerk American bills and received French francs, which she divided between the girls. "Put this money in your bags now, and be careful you don't lose it. That's about ten American dollars' worth," she explained as the girls examined the strange-looking money.

"Their bills are so much bigger than ours," Mandie commented.

"And we get so many more francs than the dollars you gave the man," Celia added.

"But it all adds up the same," Jonathan told them.

"Aren't you getting any francs?" Mandie asked Jonathan as they waited for the adults to finish their transactions at the counter.

"No," Jonathan replied. "Remember, I don't have any money."

The girls laughed.

"Imagine," Mandie said, "the son of one of the richest men in the United States doesn't have a penny to his name!"

Jonathan smiled. "Don't worry. I'll get money from my aunt and uncle. They can get it back from my father."

"And speaking of money, Jonathan," Mandie said. "Don't forget you owe us that reward for finding you when you ran away from home, remember?"

"Now wait a minute. My father offered that reward," Jonathan corrected her. "*He* owes you." Then he smiled and added, "But of course I'll see that you get it."

"We only want it to give to Mandie's kinpeople to help build the school for their children," Celia added.

"I know," Jonathan said. "And I said I would contribute to it, too, but you girls are going to have to wait until my father comes over here."

Senator Morton turned around. "In my message to Jonathan's father, I told him that you girls had found his son stowed away on the ship and that any reward should go to you two," he assured them. "He agreed to that in his reply. So don't worry about it. You'll get the money."

Mandie tried not to look too pleased. "His father must have been relieved to hear that he had run away from home and had not been kidnapped, like all the newspapers said." Turning to Jonathan, she added, "But you know, Jonathan, I still think that was a terrible thing to do, running away from home. I've been through it, and I certainly wouldn't do it again, no matter what."

"Yeah, I know," Jonathan replied, lowering his head and digging his shoe into the carpet.

Senator Morton put his hand on Jonathan's shoulder. "I know it was a bad thing to do, Jonathan, but I believe it has jolted some sense into your father," he said kindly. "I know he has always sent you away to private schools so he could spend more time with his many businesses. Maybe he'll spend some time with *you* from now on."

Jonathan smiled up at the old man. "I sure hope so, sir," he replied. "But I also hope he'll let me stay with my aunt and uncle here in Paris for a while—at least for the summer."

"Well, let's go find those relatives of yours," the senator said.

Jonathan attended school in Paris at one time, but he had never visited his aunt and uncle at their home. They had come to his school several times instead. Therefore, the boy had no idea how to find their house.

Senator Morton engaged a public carriage and asked the driver if he could locate the address. The man didn't seem to know the area where they lived but decided he could find it.

The girls had not let Jonathan know they had seen him outside with the three girls that morning. And as they rode through the streets of Paris, they were too excited to talk about anything but the city. The carriage driver took them through the grand *Arc de Triomphe*, and Jonathan related the story of Napoleon, who began building the archway that was not finished until many years later.

"This is the *Champs-Elysées*," Jonathan told them, indicating the wide avenue they were traveling. "The most expensive shops are on this street."

Mandie gazed at the ladies in exquisite fashions strolling in and out of the stores. "I don't think I want to shop here then," she said. "I don't want to spend all my money in one place."

Celia nodded. "It's good your grandmother is controlling all our money, Mandie, because I might just spend it all on French clothes," she remarked.

Mrs. Taft smiled at her. "Dear, your mother gave me money for your spending sprees here in Europe. In fact, I really don't believe you could use it all up, no matter where you shopped. So maybe we'll visit this neighborhood later."

"Oh, thank you, Mrs. Taft!" Celia said. "I didn't realize I had that much money available. But then my mother has tried to spoil me ever since . . . since we . . . lost my father last year." Her voice quivered.

"I doubt that you could ever be spoiled, dear," Mrs. Taft said. "Your mother knows you are a sensible girl, I'm sure."

"Well, I'll be glad when I get some of *my* father's money to spend," Jonathan joked.

The driver pulled the carriage to the curb, got down from his seat, and opened the door to speak to Senator

Morton. "Sir, it seems we are headed in the wrong way, so with your permission I'll turn the carriage around and go back the other direction."

"Yes, of course," Senator Morton agreed. "But let's do be quick about it. We don't want to spend the whole day looking for one address."

"Yes sir!" the driver replied, quickly closing the door and jumping onto his seat. The man rushed the horses around the square and once again they passed through the *Arc de Triomphe*. Finally the shop area gave way to a neighborhood of beautiful homes—old, sedate and grand stone structures.

Mandie gazed outside. "Oh, imagine living in one of these houses!" she exclaimed.

"When you are older, maybe you'll have one for a vacation home," Mrs. Taft said."

"Grandmother!" Mandie was shocked at the idea. "I couldn't live here in this foreign country. I wouldn't want to leave all my friends at home for people whose language I can't understand."

Everybody laughed.

"By then you will be able to speak French as well as anyone else, dear," her grandmother replied. "And by that time you'll probably be ready to travel the world. We'll see."

Mandie only frowned at the remarks.

Snowball stirred on the seat beside Mandie and stretched. Mandie had brought the red harness to put on him whenever they walked outside. "Snowball, you probably need some air," Mandie said. She held him up on the ledge of the open window, but he was frightened by that and managed to wiggle free and get back to the seat. "Well, I guess you don't want any fresh air," she said.

The driver slowed the carriage and was evidently searching for numbers on the houses. Then he pulled over and came back to the carriage door again to speak to Senator Morton. "I believe that chateau behind the wall there is the one you are looking for, sir," he said, pointing to a large building almost hidden from view.

"Then we'll go see," Senator Morton replied. "Jonathan, come with me," he said. "At least you'll know your aunt and uncle when you see them. I won't."

"Yes sir," Jonathan said. Turning to Mrs. Taft, he told her, "Ma'am, if this is the right house, I'll come back for you and the girls. I know my aunt and uncle will want to meet you all."

"All right, Jonathan," Mrs. Taft replied. "But please hurry, I don't like sitting on a public street without an escort."

The girls watched as Jonathan led the way to an iron gate in the stone wall. Senator Morton followed. Jonathan tried to open the gate, but it seemed to be locked. He reached over his head and pulled a cord, and a bell rang somewhere inside the wall.

Mandie laughed. "Well, how do you like that? A bell for your visitors to ring to let you know they've arrived."

Jonathan pulled the cord again.

"I don't believe anyone is home," Celia said.

Then as the girls watched, an old man in work clothes came along the road and walked up to the gate of the house next door.

Jonathan hurried toward him. "Sir, do you know if the Johnsons live here?" he called.

The man paused and looked at the boy but didn't answer. Then a woman came through the gate and joined the old man.

Jonathan began speaking to them in French.

The old woman spoke English in a high, shrill voice. "The Johnson people do not stay here much," she said. "I did not see them for this whole month."

"Have they moved away?" Jonathan asked.

"They did not move. Some other place they stay," the woman said as the man stood idly by. "People come all this month to look for them."

"I am their nephew," Jonathan explained as Senator Morton joined him. "I have come all the way from the United States to see them."

The woman shrugged her shoulders. "Many people from other countries look here for them also."

"Other countries?" Jonathan asked.

The woman nodded. "*Oui*, many strange-speaking people."

Senator Morton spoke up. "Ma'am, what did these people look like?"

"Many of them dark. I do not see them all," the woman said. "I hear from behind my door. I do not open my door to strange people."

The old man continued to stand there, looking from Senator Morton to Jonathan with a blank expression on his face, and the woman turned to go back through the gate.

"Do the Johnsons still work here in Paris?" Jonathan asked.

"*Oui*, they work at newspaper," the old woman replied with a nod. Then she spoke to the old man in French, and he followed her through the gate.

"Thank you, ma'am," Jonathan called after them. He and Senator Morton walked back to his aunt and uncle's gate, glanced through it, and started back to the carriage.

Mandie sighed. "Oh, goodness," she said. "I wonder where his kinpeople are."

"Maybe they're on vacation somewhere," Mrs. Taft said.

Jonathan and Senator Morton spoke with the driver of their carriage for a few moments and then came back inside.

"Well, no one is home," Jonathan said, taking his seat beside the girls.

"Yes, we heard, Jonathan," Mrs. Taft said as the senator sat down beside her. "You'll just have to stay with us until we can catch up with your aunt and uncle."

"Yes, ma'am," Jonathan agreed. "We're going by the newspaper office where they work to see if we can find out where they are."

Mandie glanced out the window and gasped. "Look there! There's that strange woman from the ship!" She pointed to another carriage parked across the road.

Everyone turned to look as the other carriage quickly drove off.

"It *was* that woman." Celia nodded.

"Yes, it was," Jonathan added.

Mrs. Taft and the senator exchanged glances.

"Too bad the carriage was headed in the opposite direction," Mandie said. "We could have followed it."

Celia shook her head. "We might have gotten lost."

"We don't have time to follow that woman," Mrs. Taft told them. "Right now we have to get back to the business district and find the newspaper building."

The driver knew where the newspaper office was located so it didn't take long to get there. Jonathan and Senator Morton went inside, and when they came out again, Mandie could tell they were disappointed.

"The office boy said they've been out of the country on an assignment for the past month," Jonathan said as he and the senator climbed back inside the carriage. "He's not sure where they are or when they'll be back."

"What shall we do?" Mrs. Taft asked the senator.

"I sent a message to Jonathan's father over the newspaper's wireless, telling him Jonathan would stay with us until we informed him further," Senator Morton replied. "The boss is also out of town, so I left the name of our hotel here and in London with the office boy, with instructions to see that the Johnsons get that information as soon as they return."

"That's the best thing to do," Mrs. Taft said. "That way we'll be free to continue with our sightseeing."

"Did you ask the newspaper boy if he knew anything about people from other countries coming to see your kinpeople?" Mandie asked Jonathan.

"No, I figured he wouldn't know anything about that," Jonathan replied. "But I do wonder who the people are that the woman next door saw."

"Another mystery," Mandie said, and smiling she added, "But I'm glad you're going to stay with us for a while at least."

"You may be sorry," Jonathan teased.

Chapter 5 / Jonathan's Disappearance

"Whew! I'm plumb out of breath!" Mandie gasped as she, Celia, and Jonathan stopped on the top landing of the Eiffel Tower. Mandie cuddled her squirming kitten, trying to settle him down.

"Me, too!" Celia added.

The three leaned against the barrier to look at Paris below.

"Oh, what a view!" Mandie exclaimed as she surveyed the town.

"You can see the way the Seine River weaves in and around the town," Jonathan told the girls. "See it, over there? Then let your eyes travel along its way, and it will go clear out of sight."

"It is a nice river, but it's nothing like the ones we have back home in North Carolina," Mandie replied. "Our rivers are clear, and they have falls rippling over huge rocks in places. I wish you could see the Nantahala River, Jonathan. I think it's the most beautiful of all rivers."

"Maybe some day I'll come and see it," he said.

Celia stepped back from the barrier. "My head is going round and round," she said. "I know now why your grandmother and the senator decided to stay on the first landing."

Mandie took her friend's hand. "Come on, Celia. We'll go back down," she said. "We've got lots of other things to see."

The three looked for the adults on the first landing, but there was no sign of them.

"They must have gone on down to the entrance," Jonathan said.

They found Mrs. Taft and Senator Morton waiting near the refreshment stand.

"Back so soon?" Mrs. Taft asked. "Do y'all want some tea or something?"

At that moment the three dark-haired girls appeared and sat down near the adults. They all smiled at Jonathan, and the youngest one said, *"Bonjour."*

Jonathan self-consciously dropped his gaze. "Hello," he muttered.

Mandie answered her grandmother. "I don't believe we want anything, Grandmother. Let's go on to Notre Dame."

As the adults stood up, Mandie turned to lead the way back to their carriage. Celia secretly smiled.

Once they were all back in the carriage and the senator had given the driver instructions, Mandie talked at a rapid pace to Celia, ignoring Jonathan.

"I think that was a great way to see all of Paris at once," Mandie said. "But I'm sorry you're afraid of heights. Snowball is, too. Did you notice how he wiggled around up there? He actually tried to scratch me when I wouldn't let him down. I left his new harness here in the carriage, but the next stop we make I'll put it on him."

Reaching for the red harness, Mandie quickly slipped

it over the kitten's head and shoulders. He tried to remove it. "Now, Snowball, if you want to walk around outside, you have to wear this thing."

"Whatever you do, Amanda, don't let Snowball get away from you," Mrs. Taft told her. "He'd be lost forever in this big city."

"I won't, Grandmother," Mandie replied. "He can't get out of this harness, and I'll hold the strap tight."

During their sightseeing that day, they encountered a few motor cars. Each time, the horses pulling their carriage snorted in protest, and the driver had trouble calming them down. But Mandie and the others saw a lot of the city. They finally grew so tired that Senator Morton suggested stopping at a sidewalk cafe. The girls were delighted.

The senator took them to a place where small, round, white tables with matching chairs covered part of the sidewalk. It was a small but noisy cafe. The customers talked loudly in French, roaring with laughter now and then.

The senator was able to get the last vacant table for them, and it was right in the middle.

"I wish I could understand what they're all saying," Mandie whispered across the table to her grandmother. "You can, Grandmother. Please translate for us."

Mrs. Taft smiled. "That young fellow over there is making a dinner appointment with the girl he's with." She nodded in his direction.

Mandie and Celia listened and watched attentively.

"And that big man over there is telling his friend about the fish he caught last weekend," Mrs. Taft continued. "It's all just normal conversation, dear."

"Ah, here is the waiter," Senator Morton said as a

small man in a white uniform approached their table. "Shall we just have something to drink and eat a good meal later?" he asked Mrs. Taft.

"Yes, I think so, maybe a few biscuits with the tea," she replied. "Is that all right with you young people?"

"Yes," the three agreed.

Senator Morton spoke to the man in French. The man bowed slightly, hurried off, and was back in a few moments with their order.

Mandie sipped the hot tea and then made a face. "Grandmother, what kind of tea is this?" she asked. "It doesn't taste so good."

Mrs. Taft laughed. "It's what the French normally drink, dear. You must put some sugar and cream in it. It'll be delicious that way."

The girls tried her suggestion and then bit into the dainty tea biscuits with a look of approval.

Mandie practically ignored Jonathan the rest of the day, even through dinner at their hotel that night. Jonathan seemed not to notice. He carried on a lively conversation with Celia most of the time.

"Are we going back to London tomorrow like we had originally planned, or are we staying here until Jonathan's kinpeople get in touch with us?" Mandie asked her grandmother across the table.

Mrs. Taft looked at the senator. "What shall we do?"

"Why don't we decide in the morning," Senator Morton replied. "We may be out rather late with the concert tonight."

"Are we going to a concert?" Mandie asked.

"Do you feel up to staying out past midnight?" Mrs. Taft asked. "People keep late hours over here, and it will undoubtedly be after midnight before the concert is over."

"Well, I believe I'd rather just stay in our rooms and write some letters and catch up with my journal," Mandie said thoughtfully. "I haven't written to my mother yet. I'll go to a concert another time after I get accustomed to this late night life."

"That sounds like a good idea." Mrs. Taft nodded. "You need to get caught up on your sleep. We'll be going to other events."

"I have a chess set in my luggage," Senator Morton spoke up. "Maybe you'd like to play some chess while we're gone."

"I don't know how to play chess, Senator Morton," Mandie said.

"I do," Celia and Jonathan spoke at the same time.

"All right then, Jonathan, you may visit the girls in their parlor for a game of chess, if you leave the hall door open," Mrs. Taft said. "You are all three to retire at your regular bedtime so you'll be fresh for tomorrow. And whatever you do, do not allow any strangers to come into our rooms."

"Yes, ma'am," the three agreed.

After an early dinner in the dining room of their hotel that night, Mrs. Taft and Senator Morton left for the concert. Jonathan set up the senator's chess set on a table in the girls' parlor, and he and Celia began teaching Mandie how to play.

Celia and Mandie joined forces against Jonathan, and Celia explained to her friend what they were doing as they made each move. Mandie found her attention wandering. This game looked too complicated.

As soon as we get done with this silly game, I've got to write to my mother, Mandie was thinking. *I hadn't realized how much I would miss my mother. Since I just found my real mother last year, I don't like being separated from her,* she thought. *I wish Mother could have come with us, but there's Samuel, that new baby brother of mine. I'll be glad when he's old enough to be left with someone else so she can go places with me.*

"Mandie, look!" Celia said excitedly. "Watch this move. I'm going to block Jonathan."

"I'm sorry," Mandie apologized, watching Celia complete the move.

"You're not too interested in this game, are you, Mandie?" Jonathan said. "Maybe we could find something else to do."

"Go ahead and finish the game," Mandie urged. "I'll just watch."

The two took up the challenge, each feeling rather confident, but it was Jonathan who finally won the match.

Mandie looked at her watch on the chain around her neck. "We have another hour before we have to go to bed," she told her friends. "What do y'all suggest?"

"Food!" Jonathan gasped with a silly grin.

"Food?" Celia repeated. "Where do we get food?"

"Jonathan, you know all about the customs in this country," Mandie said. "Is there any way we can get something for a snack?"

"Just leave it to me," Jonathan said, jumping up from his chair. "I'll just go down and raid the hotel kitchen."

"Jonathan!" Celia exclaimed. "Not really!"

"Is there any place we can buy something this late?" Mandie asked.

"Mandie, we are not to leave the hotel," Celia reminded her friend.

"We don't have to buy anything," Jonathan told the

girls. "My father has stayed at this hotel, and he has an account here. Don't worry about it. I'll be back shortly."

"What are you bringing back?" Mandie asked.

"Whatever they have in the kitchen—maybe some tea and biscuits," he said, heading for the open hallway door. He stopped short. "I would suggest you girls close this door while I'm gone," he added.

"You're right, Jonathan," Mandie said, getting up to close the door after him. "When you come back, you'll have to identify yourself before we open it."

The girls put the chess set back in its case and discussed their travels while they waited for Jonathan to return.

"We never did ask Jonathan what he was doing outside eating with those three girls this morning," Celia reminded Mandie.

"I don't intend to mention it," Mandie said. "It's his business. But I can't imagine what he was talking to them about."

"I know," Celia agreed. "I wonder if they told him who they were and where they're going."

"I plan to ignore them," Mandie said, pacing around the parlor. "If I let myself worry about the way they seem to be following us around, it'll ruin my travels over here in Europe."

"You're right, Mandie. We'll just pretend they don't even exist."

After a while Mandie looked at her watch and gasped. "Celia, Jonathan has been gone a whole hour, and it's time to go to bed. Where do you suppose he went?"

"Knowing Jonathan, there's no telling," Celia replied, getting up from her chair.

Snowball suddenly came bounding out of their bedroom. Mandie laughed. "Snowball, it's time to go to bed, not get up." She stooped to talk to her white kitten. "You shouldn't have been napping ever since dinner. Now you'll want to roam around the room all night." Snowball meowed in reply and then sat down to wash his face.

About thirty minutes later, the girls were really beginning to get worried. Jonathan should have been back long ago.

"Do you suppose Jonathan couldn't get any food and just went on back to his own room since it's bedtime?" she asked.

"Surely he would let us know," Celia replied.

"I tell you what," Mandie said. "I'll just step across the hall and knock on his door. You stand here in our doorway and watch for me."

"All right, but please make it fast," Celia said, going to the door with Mandie.

No one answered Mandie's knock on the door of Senator Morton's suite. While Celia watched, Mandie pushed open the unlocked door, poked her head inside the room, and called his name. "Jonathan! Jonathan! Are you in here?" she called.

Suddenly a uniformed maid appeared from within the bedrooms of the suite. "Whom do you seek, mademoiselle?" she asked. "I make the beds ready."

"I wondered why the door was unlocked," Mandie told the girl. "Is there anyone here? I'm looking for Jonathan."

The maid shook her head and came forward. "There is no one here."

As Mandie stepped back across the hall, the maid smiled at her and went on down the corridor. The girls went back inside to their parlor and closed the door.

"I wish Jonathan would hurry up and come back,"

Mandie said, stomping her foot. Suddenly a terrible thought struck her. "Celia, do you suppose Jonathan has run away again?" she asked.

"Oh, Mandie! Maybe he has," Celia replied as the two girls sat down on the settee. "But then, why would he do such a thing?"

"Maybe he's afraid his father will come over here and take him home," Mandie suggested. "But where would he go? His aunt and uncle aren't home, and no one knows where to find them."

"Mandie, shouldn't we just go to bed?" Celia urged. "It's past our bedtime, and your grandmother told us—"

"I know," Mandie interrupted. "But I consider this an emergency. How can we just go to bed, not knowing what's happened to Jonathan? I think we'd better wait up and see if he comes back."

"Of course," Celia agreed with a sigh. "I just don't want your grandmother to be angry with us."

"Grandmother's more likely to be angry with Jonathan if he's not back by the time she and Senator Morton return from the concert," Mandie said.

Snowball jumped up on the settee beside Mandie and curled up to go back to sleep.

"We could go find the kitchen and see if Jonathan has been there," Mandie suggested.

"No, no, Mandie," Celia objected. "It's way too dangerous."

"But how could it be dangerous?" Mandie asked. "We're on the main floor. All we'd have to do is walk up to the counter at the front door and ask where the kitchen is."

"No, Mandie," Celia protested strongly. "We might get lost and we can't even speak French. We'd better just wait here."

"I could go by myself," Mandie persisted. "And you could stay here with the door locked."

"Please, Mandie, let's not go hunting for the kitchen," Celia pleaded.

"Well, suppose I just go up to the front counter and ask somebody there if they've seen Jonathan?" Mandie asked.

No matter what Mandie suggested Celia would not agree, so Mandie finally gave up.

"Hey, Mandie," Celia said suddenly, her eyes wide. "Jonathan might have run into those three girls and gone off somewhere with them."

"That's an idea." Mandie nodded. "It would be just like him to do that."

"Well, shall we go to bed now?" Celia asked.

"No, Celia. You can if you want to, but I'm not going to bed until Jonathan comes back. Wherever he is, he ought to realize we'll wait up for him," Mandie said.

"Then I'll stay up with you, but I sure hope he comes back before your grandmother returns. She'll be awfully upset," Celia reminded her.

Mandie kept looking at her watch every now and then as they restlessly roamed about the parlor.

Finally the hands on her watch reached midnight. "It's twelve o'clock!" she cried.

"And your grandmother and the senator will be back anytime now," Celia remarked, rubbing her sleepy green eyes.

Not long after that there was a knock on the parlor door. The girls looked at each other and rushed to answer it. Just in time, Mandie remembered not to open the door. "What is it?" she called.

A man's voice outside replied, "I am the bellhop, mademoiselle. A message I have for Amanda Shaw."

The girls exchanged glances again, and Mandie slowly opened the door just enough to peek outside. A bellhop in uniform stood in the hallway.

"A message? I'm Amanda Shaw," Mandie told the young man, opening the door an inch more.

"Man in the lobby ... he has the message," the boy began, trying to sort out his English. "Madame Taft and Monsieur Morton, have accident—"

Mandie flung the door wide open. "My grandmother has had an accident?" Her heart was beating wildly. "Where is she?"

"The man in the lobby know," the bellhop replied. "Not to worry, not a bad accident, but Amanda Shaw he will take to see Madame Taft and Monsieur Morton."

Mandie quickly turned to her friend. "Let's get our wraps. Hurry!"

While the bellhop waited, the girls rushed into the bedroom and pulled their capes out of the wardrobe. Mandie snatched up Snowball and his red harness. Tears filled her eyes as the bellhop led the way to the lobby. Celia grabbed Mandie's hand and held it tightly.

"Celia, please pray that my grandmother and the senator are all right," Mandie said.

"Of course, Mandie," Celia replied. "But the bellhop said it was not a serious accident."

"It must have been serious enough that my grandmother is unable to come back to the hotel," Mandie said.

Scenes of accidents flashed through Mandie's mind as they continued down the long hallway. *Please, dear God, don't let anything happen to my grandmother or Senator Morton*, she silently prayed.

Chapter 6 / The Strange Woman From the Ship

The bellhop led Mandie and Celia into the front lobby to a tall, thin, middle-aged man with a thick mustache. Small, black, beady eyes peered out of his dark, swarthy face. He was dressed in plain olive-colored pants and a tan shirt.

Mandie rushed forward and grasped the man's sleeve. "Please, mister, what has happened to my grandmother? Please tell me!" she begged.

The bellhop and the dark man quickly exchanged words in French. Then the bellhop turned to Mandie and said, "This is Monsieur DeWeese. He is an *agent de police*—a policeman—in the plain clothes. No speak English. He say small traffic accident happen to Madame Taft and Monsieur Morton. He take you to the hospital."

"Thank you," Mandie said to the bellhop.

"*Il n'y a pas de quoi*," the bellhop replied as he bowed. "You're welcome."

The bellhop disappeared back down the long hallway, and the dark man motioned for the girls to follow him out the front door of the hotel. He had a carriage waiting in the street and indicated that Mandie and Celia should get in.

Mandie and Celia followed the man into the vehicle without question, and the drive took off at a high speed. Snowball clung to his mistress in fright as they bumped and jolted along.

"What on earth could have happened to my grandmother and the senator?" Mandie said nervously.

"The man at the hotel said it was a small accident, so maybe they're not even hurt," Celia consoled her, holding Mandie's hand. "I sure hope *we* don't have an accident the way this carriage is speeding along."

"And that Jonathan, going off like that and not even bothering to come back. Just wait till I catch up with him," Mandie threatened.

"He must have had some good reason," Celia said. "I don't think he would deliberately keep us waiting all that time."

"You know, Celia, I just thought of something—" Mandie said, glancing at the dark man sitting on the other seat. "I wish he could speak English—anyway, maybe someone told Jonathan about the accident when he left our room, and he went on to see about my grandmother and the senator. Do you think that could be why he didn't come back?"

"I just don't know, Mandie," Celia replied. "It could be. But I don't see why he wouldn't have come back and told us first."

"I suppose so, Celia. But maybe he didn't want to worry us." Her voice began to tremble as tears flooded her blue eyes. "I'm so worried about my grandmother."

Celia quickly pulled a handkerchief from her dress pocket and handed it to Mandie. "Here, Mandie, use this."

Mandie took the handkerchief and dabbed at the tears. As the speeding carriage rushed through street after street, it seemed to Mandie as though they were traveling in circles. The driver hurried around corners so fast that the girls slid around on the seat. Snowball clung to his mistress and protested with angry meows.

"Aren't we ever going to get wherever we're going?" Mandie complained as she held onto Snowball with one hand and Celia with the other.

"Paris must be an awfully big city," Celia said. "It didn't seem to be this large while we were sightseeing."

Mandie glanced at the policeman in the seat opposite them. He seemed to be listening to their conversation, but the bellhop had said the man didn't speak English. When the policeman noticed Mandie looking at him, he smiled and looked out the window into the night.

The girls suddenly realized they had left the lighted business area and had entered what seemed to be a dimly lit residential neighborhood. The carriage slowed down and came to a jerking halt in front of one of the small houses.

"This is a house, not a hospital," Mandie whispered to Celia. "The bellhop said the man would take us to the hospital."

"That's right," Celia whispered, sounding worried.

The driver opened the door of the carriage, and the dark man quickly stepped out, beckoning the girls to join him.

Mandie stayed put. "Where is the hospital?" she demanded.

The man spoke rapidly in French and reached inside to help the girls step out.

"Mandie, I don't like this at all," Celia said under her

breath, ignoring the man's offer of assistance.

Mandie stared straight at the man. "Where is my grandmother?" she persisted.

Instead of replying, the man grabbed both girls' hands and forced them to leave the carriage.

"Celia, we can't stay here," Mandie whispered in her friend's ear. "Let's run!"

Mandie managed to break loose from the man, but he tripped her, and she stumbled and fell. Snowball whined loudly in protest as he clung to Mandie's cape.

Celia seemed frozen as she stood watching. Then as she reached out to help her friend rise from the road, the man grabbed Mandie's hand again.

Mandie dragged her feet as the man forced her and Celia toward the house. The sky was extremely dark compared to the lighted streets of Paris, and the girls had no idea where they were.

As they went through the gate in the wall around the house, someone opened the front door, and waited for them. When the girls came closer, the figure came forward and put an arm around each girl.

"How are you, dears?" the female voice said, leading them inside into the lamplight.

Without speaking, the man turned and left.

The girls both looked up in shock. It was the strange woman from the ship!

Mandie exploded in anger. "You again! What do you want with us?" she demanded as the woman carefully locked the front door.

The woman in black smiled. "Sit down," she told them, pointing toward a settee in the room. "Make yourselves comfortable. You have a long wait."

Mandie stomped her foot. "Where is my grandmother?" she asked angrily. "That man who brought us here said my grandmother and the senator had an accident and that he would take us to them." She looked around the dim room. "He also said he was a policeman, but he wasn't, was he?"

"Now, now, dear, don't get so excited," the woman said sweetly. "How could that man say anything to you when he doesn't speak English and you don't speak French?"

"He didn't tell me directly, but that's what the bellhop at the hotel told us," Mandie replied, refusing to sit down.

"He did," Celia affirmed.

"Do sit down, dears," the woman insisted as she stood waiting. "You see, you will have to wait here until the doctors say you can see your grandmother and the senator. You could have a long wait."

"Why? I want to know why," Mandie persisted.

"That's the way they do things here in Paris," the woman explained, fingering the expensive-looking brooch she always wore. "Even though it was a minor accident, the patients cannot have visitors until the doctors give permission. Now I can guarantee you that your grandmother and the senator are not seriously injured."

"I am going back to the hotel," Mandie said emphatically. She started toward the front door, and Celia followed.

The woman jumped ahead of her, took the key out of the lock, and put it in her pocket. "You will wait right here, dear," the woman said, smiling.

"If you don't let us go, you'll be sorry," Mandie said, mustering all the confidence she could. "My grandmother has a lot of influence."

"I know very well who your grandmother is, dear," the

woman replied. "Now why don't you two sit down like young ladies, and as soon as the doctors give permission, I'll take you to see Mrs. Taft and the senator."

"Just how are you involved in this charade?" Mandie asked. "I don't believe my grandmother had any kind of accident. You're up to something. I remember you from the ship. You were always following us around. Why are you so interested in us?"

The woman ignored her questions but kept smiling. "If you young ladies would just sit down, we could discuss this matter," she insisted.

Celia nudged her friend. "We can't leave, Mandie, so we might as well sit down," she whispered.

"All right, we'll sit down, but we're not staying long," Mandie said to the woman. She and Celia sat on the edge of a small settee. Snowball curled up in Mandie's lap. But instead of going to sleep as he usually did, he kept his eyes on the strange woman.

The woman took a chair nearby. "Now, would you young ladies like some tea?" she asked.

"We don't want anything you've got, Mrs.— What is your name, anyway?" Mandie replied.

"My name is not important," the woman said. "I'm sorry you won't have tea. Perhaps you'd like to lie down while you wait for word from the doctor." She got up and started toward a hallway with a door visible to the parlor. Pushing open the door, she called back to the girls, "Come along, young ladies, and get some rest."

Mandie didn't answer the woman, but whispered to Celia, "Let's go in there where we can talk." She got up and Celia followed.

The room was meagerly furnished with a bed, a bureau, and a chair. Everything looked old and dilapidated, except for an electric lamp on the bureau. The woman stepped over and turned it on.

"Make yourselves comfortable," the woman said. "I'll be right out here in the parlor, and I'll call you when the doctor says you can see your grandmother." She left the room, closing the door behind her.

Mandie carefully tried the doorknob. She sighed with relief to find that the woman had not locked the door. She put Snowball on the bed and sat down next to him.

Celia joined her. "Mandie, what have we got ourselves into?" she said, nervously pulling her cape around her shoulders.

"I can't figure it out," Mandie said. "I just wish I knew who that woman is, and why she would be following us all the time. And have you noticed how friendly she tries to be with us? What does she want?"

Celia shook her head. "I sure don't know. After all that nosing around on the ship, trying to make trouble for us. . . ."

The girls continued talking in hushed tones. "Celia, I'm really worried about my grandmother," Mandie confided. "And the senator, too, of course. I know I said I didn't believe the story about the accident, but I really don't know *what* to believe. I wish somebody would hurry up and come for us."

"Maybe they're not hurt, or they may not have even been in an accident," Celia told her friend.

"I know. It's just that I thought we'd have a wonderful vacation in Europe, and look at all the mysterious things that have happened. Remember that note I found in my journal when we took the ferryboat across the English Channel? It said, 'Be careful in Paris.' Someone was trying to warn me of something, but who in the world could it have been?"

"I suppose we haven't been careful enough since we got to Paris," Celia replied softly.

"If somebody doesn't come for us pretty soon, I think we'd better try to find a way out of this house," Mandie whispered.

"But how will we find the way back to the hotel?" Celia asked.

Mandie thought for a minute. "I spent all my money on presents for my mother and my Uncle John while we were sightseeing. Do you have any money left for a carriage?" she asked.

Celia opened her drawstring bag and held up two coins. "This is all I have, and I don't think they're worth much."

Mandie examined them. "These are British pennies," she said, disappointed.

"Right," Celia replied. "I got them at the hotel in London to keep for souvenirs. But wouldn't the people here in Paris accept them?"

"I don't think so since every country has its own money," Mandie said. "Even if they would, those pennies aren't worth enough to hire a carriage. Oh, what can we do?"

"Don't forget Jonathan should have returned by now and he'll come looking for us, especially if your grandmother and the senator haven't returned from the concert," Celia suggested. "And if they're back, they'll definitely be looking for us."

"But how could they find us?" Mandie sighed. "Celia, I think we'd better say our verse. We need some help." Reaching for her friend's hand, she held it tightly as they repeated together, " 'What time I am afraid, I will put my trust in Thee.' "

"Now let's just wait for something to happen," Mandie said.

Hours dragged by, and the girls refused to lie down, afraid they would go to sleep. They wanted to be awake in case anyone came for them. They leaned against each other for support as they sat on the bed until sleep finally overcame them.

Some time later they both woke with a start and then realized where they were. "Sh-h-h!" Mandie cautioned Celia as they rubbed their eyes. They listened but couldn't hear a sound.

Mandie got up to examine the windows in the room. They were all tightly sealed. It would be impossible to open one. The girls' only way out would be through the door, which was in clear view of the woman in the parlor.

Celia crept quietly over to the door, opened it enough to peek out, and then closed it again. "She's reading— but she's also wide awake," Celia reported.

"If she'd just doze off, I think we could get past her and try to find some way out of this house," Mandie said. "She has the door key in her pocket, but there might be another way."

The girls pulled back the heavy, coarse draperies and sat on the edge of the bed facing the windows. As they waited, the first streaks of dawn began to light up the sky. Mandie softly opened the door and saw that the woman had finally fallen asleep on the settee.

She quickly picked up Snowball from the bed and motioned for Celia to follow her. The house was still dark except for the parlor and the room they had been in. They had to move slowly to keep from bumping into something and waking the woman.

The girls checked each window they came to, but

they were all secured. The house was much larger than it had seemed from the road, and there were many rooms to search for a way out.

Finally, arriving at the back door, Mandie examined it and sighed. "Locked—with two different locks. You must need a key for this one, too." In frustration, she looked around in the dim light coming though the thin curtains. "Look!" She pointed. "There's another door. Let's try it."

Mandie hurriedly turned the doorknob. To the amazement of them both, it opened! As Mandie slowly pushed open the creaking door, she could barely see steps descending into complete darkness. "It's the cellar!" she whispered to Celia.

"We aren't going down there, are we?" Celia protested, peering into the darkness. "There may be rats!"

"It's our only hope," Mandie answered. "We've got to at least find out what's down there," Mandie said, clutching her squirming kitten. "Besides, if there are any rats, they won't bother us because they'll be afraid of Snowball."

"Oh, I wish I had never come to Europe," Celia moaned.

"Come on," Mandie urged. "I'll go first. Be careful and don't fall. You could get hurt."

Mandie slowly felt her way down the stairs with Celia holding onto the back of Mandie's skirt. As they reached the bottom step, the girls looked around. It was dark down there, but there was enough light from somewhere that they could distinguish supplies stacked here and there.

"We have to be awfully quiet," Mandie whispered in Celia's ear. "We may be directly under the parlor, and that woman might wake up."

"Right," Celia said, hardly breathing.

They moved slowly around the large room and found several smaller rooms. In one of these, Mandie spotted a window. "Look!" she whispered, hurrying to examine it. The window was too high for her to reach.

Silently, they looked around for something to stand on. Finding a heavy barrel in the corner, they struggled to place it beneath the window. It took every ounce of their strength, but they finally succeeded. They stopped to catch their breath.

Mandie had to put Snowball down in order to move the barrel, but he stayed close to her feet until they reached the window with it. As the girls rested a moment, the white kitten jumped up on the barrel and then in a flying leap landed on the window sill above. Turning to look out the window, he immediately puffed up his fur and meowed angrily.

"Sh-h-h! Snowball, be quiet," Mandie whispered. Climbing on top of the barrel, she stood on tiptoe to look through the window. She tried to open it, but it wouldn't move. She couldn't see a lock, but something was holding it.

Celia watched from below. "Will it open?" she whispered.

Mandie felt around the window sash. "It's not locked, but I can't open it." Suddenly her fingers felt something sharp on top of the bottom sash. "Aha! I've found a tenpenny nail. It's nailed shut."

"Maybe I can find something to pry it out," Celia said, looking around the small room.

"We can't use anything that will make a noise. That woman will hear us," Mandie told her. She continued pushing at the nail but couldn't budge it. Even Snowball tried to help. He was still upset about something outside, but he also seemed interested in what his mistress was doing.

"I can't find a single thing," Celia said, searching the darkness.

"I know what." Mandie stooped down while still standing on the barrel. "Help me unbutton my shoe. I can probably loosen the nail with my shoe heel."

Together they got Mandie's shoe off, and she went to work on the nail. Managing to get the tiny shoe heel between the nail and the wood, she wiggled it back and forth and finally gave a sigh of triumph as the nail came out.

"I got it!" She whispered as she stooped to put her shoe back on. After quickly buttoning it, she stood up. "Now maybe we can get out of here."

The window was easy to open, and Mandie hoisted herself up from the barrel and through the opening. Celia followed, with Snowball rushing out ahead of them both. Once again he arched his back and puffed up his fur.

As the girls straightened up in the dim light outside, they found themselves in a thicket of bushes.

Mandie became nervous about her kitten. "Snowball, come here!" she demanded in a hoarse whisper.

Suddenly there was a loud growl and the girls froze.

"A dog!" Celia gasped, clinging to Mandie's skirt.

There on the other side of the bushes was a huge black dog, eyeing Snowball. Mandie grabbed her kitten, and when she did, the dog growled again.

Mandie passed the white kitten to her friend. "Here, you hold onto Snowball, and I'll see if I can talk this dog into letting us by," she whispered. "Please don't let Snowball get away."

Mandie turned her attention to the dog and spoke in

low tones. "Here, doggie, here. Come here, doggie."

The dog bared his teeth.

Mandie looked around quickly. "Celia, if you can get through that gap in the bushes over there while I distract the dog, maybe he'll let me through," she suggested nervously. "I have an idea he's more interested in Snowball than he is in us."

While Mandie whispered to the dog in soothing tones, Celia slowly edged away with Snowball and made it through the opening in the bushes. As soon as Snowball was out of sight, the big dog became friendly and edged forward for Mandie to pat his head.

"Doggie, I hate to do this, but I'd rather you were inside and away from us," Mandie said. "Come on, doggie. Come on." She quickly led him to the open window and snapped her fingers for him to jump through. To her amazement, he bounded through the opening, hardly making a sound as he landed on the floor below. Hastily pulling the window down, Mandie hurried to catch up with Celia.

"Where's the dog?" Celia asked as Mandie joined her on the back lawn of the house.

Mandie looked around as she took her kitten from her friend. "I put him in the cellar," she replied, noticing how much lighter it was outside now. "What do you say we go that way?" She pointed toward the yard of the house behind the one from which they had just escaped.

Mandie led the way through the yard to the high wall separating the houses, and she and Celia struggled to climb over. Making their way across the lawn of the neighboring house, they scaled its front wall and finally found themselves on the road that ran parallel to the one they had been on.

Stopping to catch their breath, Mandie decided, "There's only one way to get back to the hotel, and that is to start walking." She looked around. "This way, I think." The girls took the road uphill.

Celia shook her head. "I just hope we can find the way, Mandie," she said.

"Don't worry. We will—" Mandie promised, "—sooner or later."

Chapter 7 / Lost in Paris

Even though the sun was just coming up, the streets were already full of people rushing in every direction.

Mandie and Celia hurried along, now and then stopping someone to ask the way to the Hotel Rochambeau. But no one could understand them. The girls hastily made their way through a maze of narrow cobblestone streets lined with small dwellings and tiny shops. Dozens of poorly clad children played among the intersections of alleys while dogs and cats roamed among them. Mandie had to hold Snowball especially tight whenever they passed other cats and dogs.

"Celia, do you realize that we haven't seen a single public carriage—in fact a carriage of any kind—since we left that house?" Mandie asked as they continued their hurried pace. "This must be a poorer section of Paris. We can't be anywhere near our hotel."

"I was just thinking the same thing," Celia agreed, making long strides to keep up with her friend. "And how are we going to find our way back to the hotel when we can't even ask anyone for directions? I wish I could speak French!"

"Remember our verse, Celia," Mandie said, catching Celia's free hand in hers.

Together they recited in low tones, " 'What time I am afraid I will put my trust in Thee.' "

"Now everything will be all right, Celia. I think we need to slow down a little, though, or we'll flat give out of breath," Mandie said as she slackened her pace.

Celia suddenly stopped in her tracks and pointed to the left. "Oh, Mandie, look!" she exclaimed. "There's the Eiffel Tower."

Mandie stopped to look in the direction Celia pointed. "It is, Celia! We'll just go there. Remember, the driver told us you can find someone there who speaks almost any language. There's bound to be an American or Englishman at the tower who can understand us. I told you everything was going to be all right!"

The girls turned off onto a smaller, narrower street to the left and aimed for the Tower. With each intersection they passed, the neighborhood became cleaner and more orderly. The streets were full of carriages.

"It sure is a long way to the Tower, when it looked so close back there," Celia commented.

The girls crossed a beautiful park with blooming flowers and neat hedges. "That's because the Eiffel Tower is so tall that you can see it all over Paris," Mandie reminded her friend. "Let's stop for five minutes and rest." She plopped onto a nearby bench and Celia joined her.

"I wonder if Jonathan ever came back to the hotel," Celia said, "or I should say his room. I don't know that he ever actually left the hotel."

"Maybe he met up with those three girls—or maybe he decided to run away again," Mandie suggested as she let Snowball down to wander around while she held on to his leash. "You know something?" She laughed. "I just realized I'm hungry."

"Me, too," Celia acknowledged. "When we get back to the hotel, we can eat to our heart's content—that is, if we ever find the way."

"And don't forget about my grandmother and the senator," Mandie said. "I hope that strange woman was lying and that they didn't have an accident. The whole episode was so unbelievable, being persuaded to leave the hotel with a stranger only to end up locked up in a house with that mysterious woman. I just can't figure out what that woman was up to."

Children playing nearby threw their ball and it rolled in front of Snowball. He pounced on it and jerked the leash out of Mandie's hand.

Mandie jumped up and raced after her kitten as he chased the ball. "Snowball! Come back here!" she called.

The children watched as Mandie managed to step on the end of the leash. Snowball looked at his mistress in shock at the sudden restraint. Mandie picked him up and held him tight.

"Snowball, we just don't have time to play," she told him. "Celia, I think we'd better get on."

The girls finally arrived at the Eiffel Tower, tired, hungry, worried, and with sore feet. Lots of tourists milled around, and Mandie and Celia mingled with them, keeping an ear open for the sound of English, which was the only language they could understand. Finally they spotted an older man and woman posing for a photograph. The woman photographer was saying, "Now, please be still!"

Mandie and Celia rushed through the crowd. As soon as the photographer finished taking the picture, Mandie approached the three. They were nicely dressed and acted friendly when the girls spoke.

"Ma'am, we heard you speaking English, and we imagine you must be American," Mandie began. "We're from the United States too, but we're lost right now and can't make anyone understand what we're saying. We're trying to find our way back to the Hotel Rochambeau," she explained to the lady photographer. "Can you tell us which way to go?"

The lady looked at Mandie and Celia with concern. "Oh, dear, you mean you two are all alone?" she asked, not waiting for an answer. "Why, dears, you are not very far from your hotel, but don't you think you'd better get a carriage?"

"Well, no, ma'am," Mandie replied. "If we're nearby, we can walk. Could you just point out what direction?"

The woman pointed beyond the Tower. "You go three streets that way, and then go left," she explained. "After three streets in that direction, you turn right. From there you can see your hotel."

The girls thanked the lady and then hurried in the direction she had indicated. When they had almost covered the first three blocks, they both stopped suddenly and stared straight ahead.

"Jonathan!" Mandie gasped, pointing to a stopped carriage down the avenue. Two men were forcing Jonathan to get into the carriage.

The girls broke into a run, but they weren't fast enough. The carriage pulled away in a rush, and Mandie and Celia stopped in disappointment.

"It looked to me like those men were treating Jonathan like a prisoner or something," Mandie said, watching the carriage as it disappeared around a corner.

"They didn't look like policemen, did they?" Celia asked.

"No—they acted more like crooks!" Mandie replied, trying to soothe Snowball. "*Come on*, Celia, we've got to get back to the hotel and find out what's going on!"

When they turned the last corner and the hotel came into view, the girls practically ran the rest of the way. They rushed through the crowded lobby and down the long hallway to their rooms.

Mandie tapped on the door. "Grandmother," she called anxiously, "it's me, Mandie."

There was no answer. Mandie tried the knob and the door opened. The girls ran into the suite and looked around. There was no one there.

Mandie began to feel worried again. "Grandmother!" she called out, looking into both bedrooms. "Celia, let's go ask the man at the counter if he's seen my grandmother."

The girls turned to leave the suite and almost collided with Mrs. Taft and Senator Morton.

Mrs. Taft gasped. "Amanda! Celia!" she cried. "Where in this world have you two girls been?" She dropped onto the settee in the parlor and the senator stood beside her.

Mandie threw off her bonnet. "Grandmother, you're all right!" she cried with relief as she set Snowball down.

Mandie's grandmother looked puzzled as Mandie sat on the carpet at her knee. Celia sat down too, and removed her bonnet.

"Oh, Grandmother, we've been through some terrible things," Mandie began. "We were told you and the senator had an accident and it must have been all lies! Thank goodness, you're both all right." She laid her head against her grandmother's knee.

"Amanda, explain yourself!" Mrs. Taft told her. "What are you talking about?"

As Mandie related what had happened to them, Celia filled in details now and then. Mrs. Taft and the senator silently exchanged worried glances.

"It was awful, Grandmother, not knowing for sure whether you and Senator Morton had really had an accident," Mandie concluded.

"That woman from the ship needs to be questioned by the police," Senator Morton remarked.

"Amanda, we already have the police looking for you and Celia and Jonathan," Mrs. Taft said. "When we came back last night from the concert and couldn't find any of you, we alerted the police right away."

"Oh, Grandmother, we saw Jonathan on our way here today," Mandie added, explaining what they had seen.

"Sounds like it might be a kidnapping," Senator Morton spoke up.

"Oh dear," Mrs. Taft sighed, "Jonathan was in our care, and now it looks as though he has disappeared."

"Could you girls show us the way to the house where the man took y'all last night?" Senator Morton asked.

Mandie and Celia looked at each other and shook their heads. "We seemed to be going around in circles when the man took us there, and then when we tried to find the way back, we just went up one street and down another without any sense of direction until we spotted the Tower."

"We'd better get the police to hear what you girls have told us," Senator Morton said, going toward the door. "There is a policeman stationed in the lobby now. I'll get him."

Mrs. Taft looked at the girls with concern. "Why did

you believe such a story and agree to go off with a complete stranger?" she asked.

Tears filled Mandie's blue eyes. "Grandmother, I was worried sick, afraid that you had had an awful accident," she said. "I just wasn't thinking clearly. It was all such a shock to be suddenly told such a thing. I'm sorry."

Mrs. Taft reached out to pat Mandie's tangled blonde hair. "Amanda, you've done wrong going off like that with a stranger, but I can't bring myself to punish you for it. I might have done the same thing under the same circumstances. However, let me emphasize this right now— *never* go off anywhere with a stranger for *any* reason whatever. And never believe what a stranger tells you."

"I'm sorry, Grandmother, but we thought the man was really a policeman, and we thought we could trust a policeman," Mandie explained, wiping her tears. "I've really learned a lesson this time. I'll always be careful from now on to get identification from strangers, even policemen."

When Senator Morton returned with the French policeman, he introduced him as Monsieur La Motte. The officer thoroughly questioned the girls, but there was not much information to go on. It would be an almost impossible task to find Jonathan or to locate the house to which the girls had been taken.

"And regarding the strange woman you girls describe, who was also on your ship, I'd say she was from the United States." The policeman spoke excellent English without much of an accent. "I don't believe that line takes on passengers between the U.S. and England."

"It's true we didn't make any other stops," Senator Morton affirmed.

Monsieur La Motte nodded. "I'd like you girls to contact me immediately if you ever see that woman again," he said. "Tell us exactly where you saw her and which way she was headed. Maybe if we work fast enough, we can catch her."

"Do you think she's a criminal?" Mandie asked.

"Taking you girls like she did makes her a criminal," he said, "But the only way we can question her is to find her and take her into custody."

"She tried to be so friendly with us," Celia remarked. "And on the ship she was the exact opposite."

"That's right," Mandie added. "She didn't hurt us. She just wanted us to stay there for some reason."

"Young ladies, it's hard to know what she had in mind," the policeman told them. "We are just glad you were able to escape before something terrible happened."

Mrs. Taft spoke up. "I should have gone to the captain of the ship and found out who the woman was," she said. "But I thought she was just some harmless busybody."

"What about Jonathan, Monsieur La Motte?" Mandie asked, finally getting up the nerve to say the man's name. She wasn't sure how to pronounce it.

The policeman smiled at Mandie. "We will alert the entire force across Paris and the surrounding communities," he assured her, "but I can say now that it will probably be impossible to locate him."

"Then perhaps I'd better telegraph his father," Senator Morton suggested.

"Yes, I think you should," the policeman agreed.

"His father has his own network of security men, and they can get busy on the search as well," Senator Morton said. "He is so wealthy that he keeps detectives on his payroll. One thing I don't understand about Lindall Guyer, though, is the fact that he has never given his son any protection when there are so many cases of children of wealthy businessmen being kidnapped."

"Monsieur La Motte, please try real hard to find Jonathan," Celia begged. "I think he's a good boy. It's just that his father doesn't love him."

Mandie gasped. "Celia, you can't say that because you don't know for sure. We know his father neglects him, but we don't know that he doesn't love him."

"Well, if I loved someone I'd want to protect him," Celia reasoned.

The policeman spoke again. "I understand what you young ladies are saying. We will do everything we can to find him. Now I must go and begin the search."

When Monsieur La Motte left, Mrs. Taft and the senator rose from their seats, and Mrs. Taft told the girls, "You girls get a bath now, and I'll have some food brought in for you. Then y'all need to take a long nap."

Mandie protested, "Grandmother, couldn't we help look for Jonathan?" she begged. "He may be in terrible danger!"

"This may be a dangerous situation," Mrs. Taft replied. "Therefore, I am forbidding you girls to get mixed up in it in any way. Is that understood?"

"Yes, ma'am," the girls replied meekly in unison.

"You know, Mrs. Taft, that policeman didn't even ask us for a description of the carriage that took Jonathan away," Celia remarked.

"Well, aren't all carriages more or less alike, dear?" Mrs. Taft replied, smiling. "I don't see how one could differentiate between them."

Mandie suddenly remembered something. "Grandmother, the carriage that picked up Jonathan *was* different. Well, not the carriage . . . but the horses. They had unusually big feet—or hoofs."

"They were Clydesdale horses, Mandie, bred in Scotland," Celia told her. "We have some on our farm in Virginia."

"Well, whatever they were, the carriage that picked up Jonathan had that kind of horses pulling it." Mandie sounded very certain.

Senator Morton had been listening and now he remarked, "Yes, that is unusual for Clydesdales to be hitched to a carriage," he said, "especially here in Paris. I'll pass that information on to Monsieur La Motte if I can catch him before he leaves the hotel."

The senator quickly left, and Mrs. Taft ushered the girls into the room to get baths while she went to order food.

Snowball curled up on the bed contentedly, while the girls bathed and put on clean clothes.

Mandie's thoughts raced as she brushed out her long blonde hair. "I do hope the policemen can find that woman," she said. "She may cause us trouble again if someone doesn't stop her. And I would imagine that she's mixed up in abducting Jonathan."

"Well, thank the Almighty that we were able to get away," Celia remarked as she pulled on fresh stockings.

"We're going to have to see what we can do to help rescue Jonathan," Mandie mused.

"Mandie, your grandmother has forbidden us to get mixed up in anything, remember?" Celia replied.

"I didn't say we'd get mixed up in anything," Mandie protested. "There must be some way we can help find him, though."

Chapter 8 / Spies in the Palace

Mandie and Celia had a late breakfast with Mrs. Taft and Senator Morton in the hotel dining room, and Mrs. Taft told them about some people in Paris who had become close friends during her frequent trips there.

"Lorraine Lafayette has two daughters about your ages, and the girls would like for you to visit them so they can show you their city," Mrs. Taft said between sips of coffee.

Mandie buttered a roll. "It would be interesting to meet some French girls," she said. "When could we go, Grandmother?"

"Well, I told Lorraine that if she would pick you girls up this morning the Senator and I could go to another friend's home for a luncheon she is giving," Mrs. Taft said. "There won't be any young people at the luncheon, you see."

"Oh, yes, Mrs. Taft, I'd like that," Celia agreed.

"What about Jonathan?" Mandie asked. "What if there's some word from the police? Shouldn't we stay close to the hotel today?"

Senator Morton spoke up. "I have already taken care

of that," he said. "I have left word at the hotel desk where the police can find us in case there is any news."

"Then I'll go," Mandie said.

"I will, too," Celia added.

"Then it's all settled," Senator Morton said. "We'll be back before it's time for you to return."

The adults had finished their breakfast while the girls dallied over theirs.

Mrs. Taft folded her napkin. "Can I trust you girls to wait here for Mrs. Lafayette so the senator and I can leave?" she asked.

"Of course, Grandmother," Mandie agreed.

"Mrs. Lafayette will come to the front desk to ask for y'all, so you need to be ready and waiting in the lobby—" She looked at her watch pinned on her jacket. "—in about thirty or forty minutes."

"That'll give us time to finish getting ready," Mandie assured her. She bent to set a saucer under the table for Snowball, who was tied to the table leg with his leash. "Here, Snowball, eat this bacon before we leave."

The kitten meowed and eagerly bit into the meat.

Mrs. Taft and the senator rose to leave the room. "I hope y'all have a nice time, dears," Mrs. Taft said. "We'll be back late this afternoon before y'all return."

As soon as the adults left, the girls hastily finished their breakfast. "I need to hurry and take Snowball outside for some air before we go off with those people," Mandie said. "Come to think of it, I forgot to ask Grandmother if I could take him with me today."

"You take him everywhere, Mandie, and now that you have the leash, I don't think anyone would object," Celia said. She finished the last bite of her eggs.

"I'll just ask Mrs. Lafayette when she gets here," Mandie decided. The girls finished and hurried through the lobby to the front door.

Mandie pushed the big door open and gasped. "Celia! Look! There's the carriage with the Clydesdale horses!" She pointed to a vehicle parked just past the doorway.

"That's it all right," Celia said.

"Let's see who's in it," Mandie said as she and Celia hurried into the street. But just as they reached it, the carriage suddenly lurched off down the road.

Passengers were alighting from a public carriage in front of the hotel, and Mandie stepped up to the driver. "Can you take us to follow that carriage?" she called, pointing to the vehicle down the road.

"*Oui*, mademoiselle," the man agreed. "Yes, get in."

The girls quickly got inside and hung out the open window, trying to see ahead as their driver raced after the other vehicle. Snowball clung to Mandie's dress to keep from being thrown around.

"Mandie, do you have any money?" Celia asked as they bounced along. Mandie held up her drawstring bag and smiled. "I have lots of money this time."

"I have some, too. I just hope we have enough to pay this driver. It's so hard to figure out the difference between dollars and francs," Celia said.

"They've turned off onto another road," Mandie said as Celia watched over her shoulder. "I don't believe we've been down this road before."

"We're getting out into the country, Mandie!" Celia exclaimed. "There's no telling how far they're going."

The lush green countryside unfolded along the way. Country chateaux could be seen occasionally between the more modest farms with their summer crops.

"Our driver is keeping up with the other one all right,"

Mandie remarked as they sped along. "I hope the other driver doesn't realize we're following him."

"There are lots of carriages going up and down this road," Celia observed. "I don't think he will notice us."

After a long time the other carriage slowed and turned through a gate in the wall surrounding a huge structure. The girls' driver stopped his vehicle nearby and came back and opened the door for the girls. "Here we are, mademoiselle," the man said to Mandie. "Is this where you wanted to go?"

"Yes, thanks. Now how much do we owe you?" Mandie asked as she and Celia got down from the carriage and looked around.

"Now let me see," the driver said, watching as Mandie drew a wad of French bills out of her bag. "How much do you have there, mademoiselle?" he asked.

"I don't rightly know, sir," Mandie said, flipping through the francs.

The man silently watched and then reached out his hand. "You have enough," he said.

"You mean you want all of this money?" Mandie asked, surprised.

"*Oui*, mademoiselle." The man smiled as he took the bills.

Celia spoke up. "Mandie, how are we going to get back to town?"

"Oh, I never even thought of that," Mandie said. She turned to the driver. "How much would you charge to wait for us?"

"But you do not have any more money, mademoiselle," the man said.

"I have," Celia said, pulling bills out of her bag. "Is this enough?"

"That would be enough to wait, mademoiselle, but then you would not have enough to go back to town," the driver explained.

"Oh, goodness," Mandie moaned. She turned to the man and said, "Never mind then. We'll find some other way back. Where are we, anyhow?"

"This is the Palace Versailles," the man said, indicating the huge structure behind the walls. "It was built by Louis XIV to get away from the noise of Paris. Marie Antoinette lived here when she was Queen of France."

"Marie Antoinette!" the girls exclaimed. They had studied about her in their history classes back home in school.

"*Oui*, she was executed," the man said. "Now I must bid you good day. *Merci*." Bowing slightly, he climbed back up on his seat and drove off.

The girls managed to mutter a goodbye as their eyes took in the sight before them.

Mandie stood there on the road uncertain about what to do next. "This *is* a palace," she said with a shrug. "There must be people living in it. Should we just walk through that gate where the other carriage went and see if we can find it?" she asked, surveying the thick wall.

Celia nervously twisted the strings on her bag. "I suppose we'll have to in order to find out where they went," she replied. "I hope we don't get in trouble."

"Come on," Mandie urged her as she held on to Snowball and walked toward the gate. Celia followed.

To the girls' surprise there was a little gate house just inside the gate, and a young man in a uniform stood inside. When he saw the girls, he stepped outside and spoke rapidly to them in French.

The girls looked at him, puzzled.

"I'm sorry, but we don't understand French," Mandie said. "Do you speak English?"

The young man evidently didn't understand Mandie. Once again he spoke in French. This time he gestured toward the huge palace in the distance.

Mandie shrugged. "May we go in there?" She motioned to herself and Celia and then pointed toward the palace.

The young man in the uniform gave up, shook his head in bewilderment, and waved for them to go on in. Mandie and Celia smiled sweetly at him and continued on their way.

"Look at the doorway!" Mandie exclaimed as they neared a huge double-door entrance to the palace. "It's so big you could practically move our whole hotel right in through the door!"

"And look at those flowers! And the water fountains!" Celia squealed in delight.

"Imagine living in a place like this!" Mandie cried.

"Imagine Marie Antoinette going in and out that door!" Celia exclaimed. "I can just see her."

There were lots of other people walking about the courtyard and going in and out of the main palace building. The girls slowly moved on, drinking in all the beauty of Versailles.

Mandie blinked and turned around, looking around the front grounds. "Celia, I just realized something," she said. "I don't see any carriages anywhere. I wonder where the one pulled by the Clydesdales went."

"Well, we know it came in here," Celia replied, "and unless there's a back gate, it has got to be here somewhere."

At that moment they were almost run down by a carriage that came flying through the courtyard from behind the palace. They clutched each other in sudden fright. The vehicle quickly disappeared through the front gate.

Mandie took a deep breath and tried to calm her squirming kitten. "Evidently there's a place in the backyard for the carriages. Come on," she said. The girls quickened their pace.

As they finally got around the side of the huge palace, smaller structures came into view, along with green lawn with flowers and statues and water fountains. There were places to sit here and there.

Celia paused to look around. "Oh, I just love this place!" she said excitedly.

"It's beautiful," Mandie agreed, "but it's too big. I wouldn't want to live here." She looked over a low wall. "Celia, there are carriages down there, lots of them," she said. "Come on."

The girls hurried over the wall and surveyed the vehicles, all of which had drivers and horses waiting in the shade. They quickly examined the animals hitched to each vehicle. Several of the drivers lounging around the carriages tipped their hats and spoke in French to the girls. Mandie and Celia smiled and kept moving.

"There aren't any Clydesdales here," Celia said.

"There must be another place for the carriages, then," Mandie decided. "Let's walk on around the building."

Eventually they reached the front of the palace again without finding any more carriages. They had circled the building from a distance.

"Let's get closer to the palace and see if there's an entrance for the carriages to go inside," Mandie suggested.

Celia laughed. "Carriages—inside the palace? Oh, Mandie!"

"But, Celia, back in the old days, according to history books, carriages and horses sometimes had rooms attached to the houses," Mandie explained.

"But this is a fancy palace, Mandie," Celia argued as they glanced around.

"It's also ancient. Can't you just see Marie Antoinette riding up in her carriage and going right on into the palace in it?" Mandie asked, dreamily staring at the huge, ornate building. "Then the driver would jump down, throw open the door, and bow."

"And he would say, 'Home again, your Majesty!', and Louis XVI would be waiting inside for her," Celia added.

"Didn't they come to a terrible end—the poor king and queen?" Mandie sighed. "I've never heard of a president in our country being executed."

"But we've never had a president betray our country either," Celia reminded her.

As they stood there staring at the palace, a carriage suddenly emerged from inside the building and hurried toward the gate in the front wall.

Both girls gasped.

"I told you, Celia!" Mandie exclaimed, hurrying toward the place the vehicle had come from. "Come on. Let's go look."

As they got closer, they could see a tunnel-like opening in the building. Tall shrubbery partially hid the passageway, and they saw a guard there in a little open room.

"Oh, shucks!" Mandie said as she spotted the uniformed man.

"What are we going to do?" Celia asked as they paused halfway down the incline. "We can't speak

French, and if he talks to us, we won't know what he's saying."

"There's only one thing to do. Just try," Mandie said, leading the way. Snowball clung to the shoulder of her cape.

As the girls approached the man in uniform, they smiled at him and kept going. To their amazement the man merely smiled back and called, *"Bonjour."*

They quickly walked past him.

"Hurry!" Mandie whispered to Celia as they stepped into the passageway.

"My legs won't go any faster!" Celia whispered back. "They're too scared!"

Along the way there were doors, all closed, and no one in sight. There was not a sound anywhere. Several other passageways crossed the one they were in at various places, but they continued straight ahead.

"Do you suppose we should explore some of those other tunnels?" Celia whispered. "They're all big enough for a carriage to go through."

"I think we ought to see where this one goes first. We can always come back and try those," Mandie replied, leading the way.

As they followed a curve, the passageway grew dimmer and dimmer until it was hard to see where they were going.

"They don't have any lights down here," Mandie muttered as she and Celia joined hands.

Snowball clung to her shoulder and meowed softly.

"Sh-h-h! Snowball, be quiet!" Mandie whispered. She rubbed her cheek against his fur, and he began purring.

They had to walk slower now because it was getting harder to see the floor. Although there were no steps, they seemed to be going downhill. The air had become cool and damp smelling.

"Mandie, don't you think we ought to go back?" Celia asked softly, staying close to her friend.

"Not till we see where this goes," Mandie whispered. "Any minute now we'll probably come out in the open daylight. That carriage had to come from somewhere."

"But it could have come from one of those other tunnels we passed," Celia reminded her.

"If we don't come to an end pretty soon, we'll turn around and go back," Mandie promised.

Mandie couldn't see anything clearly on either side of them. She thought they passed a closed door now and then, but it was so dark they had to watch their feet to keep from falling as the cobblestone floor kept going downhill.

Suddenly, there was a loud clanking sound. The girls jumped and clung to each other.

"What was *that*?" Celia cried.

Before Mandie could reply, there was another bang. She grabbed Celia's hand. "Sounds like a metal gate being closed or something," she whispered. "Let's go see."

Celia refused to move forward. "Mandie, please," she whispered in a shaky voice. "I don't want to go any farther. Let's go back, *real fast*, please!"

"Then I'll go by myself," Mandie said, her heart pounding. Letting go of Celia's hand, she moved forward.

"No, Mandie, don't leave me here," Celia pleaded. She grasped Mandie's hand again. "I'll go with you."

The clanking sounds continued ahead of them. Mandie stopped. Then a male voice coming from behind them burst into song.

Mandie tugged Celia's hand, quickly pulling her over to the side of the tunnel. "Sh-h-h!" she warned.

At that moment a huge figure came striding down the passageway. The girls clung to each other as the man passed by them.

Mandie squeezed Snowball tightly, and he meowed loudly in protest.

Mandie's heart turned over, but the man once again burst into song and hurried on his way. As soon as he was out of sight, the girls relaxed again.

"Oh, Mandie," Celia breathed with relief.

"He looked like a giant, didn't he?" Mandie said.

"Yes, a mean giant!" Celia replied, trembling.

Mandie continued forward. "Come on, let's go."

"Are we going where he went?" Celia asked.

"We'll find out where he went. It may be the same place we're looking for," Mandie said. "Come on." She tugged at Celia's hand.

Celia let herself be propelled forward. "I do hope we find some daylight soon, or at least some lights." She sighed.

They caught up with the man unexpectedly as they came around a curve in the passageway. It was lighter in the distance, and they could make out the outline of the man. He seemed to be opening and closing doors along the way. The girls stopped and watched, huddling against the wall.

"W-What do y-you suppose he's—he's d-doing?" Celia asked, her teeth chattering.

"Let's get closer," Mandie whispered.

She pulled Celia's hand again, and moved on, staying close to the wall.

Suddenly the man slammed a door, and the girls

knew the source of the clanking sounds they'd heard. As they watched, he turned a big key in the lock. Then he continued down the passageway.

The girls waited for him to disappear at the far end.

"Now!" Mandie whispered, pulling Celia forward. "Let's see what's down there."

As the girls crept toward the door the man had just locked, there was a sudden loud wail. They froze in their tracks. The sound echoed through the passageway, and then there was complete silence.

After a moment of silent waiting, Mandie urged Celia forward again.

Again a loud wail echoed through the walls. "There's someone locked in that room," Mandie whispered, "and I think we ought to see who it is."

Forgetting all caution, Mandie rushed forward and tried the door. She shook it, but it wouldn't open.

"Mandie!" Celia warned. "Someone is going to hear you!"

Mandie ignored her friend. "I wish I could see through that door," she fussed.

"Please, let's go," Celia begged, shivering with fright.

Small window openings high on the walls gave a faint light in the passageway, making the place more bearable. Mandie examined every inch of the metal door, and looking around she realized that there were similar doors along the walls on both sides.

"Celia, this must be the dungeon!" she exclaimed.

"Dungeon?" Celia asked in a hoarse whisper.

"You know, *dungeons*—like they had in the old castles in our history books," Mandie replied. "The place where they kept prisoners."

"Mandie, let's get out of here!" Celia begged again.

"Someone might lock *us* up."

Mandie stooped to examine the lock on the door. The keyhole was huge. She pressed her eye against the hole, and her heart raced. "Celia!" she cried. "Jonathan's inside here! I can just barely see him, but I *know* it's Jonathan!"

"Jonathan? What are we going to do?" Celia whispered.

"We've got to get this door open somehow," Mandie said with new determination.

"But we don't have the key!" Celia argued. "How are we going to open it?"

"We'll just have to figure out something," Mandie said. "We've got to get Jonathan out of there before someone comes."

In the distance they could hear the man singing again.

Chapter 9 / The Three Dark-Haired Girls

Mandie handed Snowball to Celia and stooped again to peek through the big keyhole of the iron door. Then she put her mouth right up to the keyhole. "Jonathan! Jonathan!" she whispered loudly. "Jonathan, it's Mandie . . . and Celia!"

She looked through the small opening again, but it was impossible to see the entire room. Jonathan lay curled up on an old quilt in a corner.

"You know, Celia, he looks like he's asleep, but I don't believe he is. That must have been him we heard yell out a while ago," Mandie said, straightening up. "You look through the keyhole and see what you think."

Celia quickly peeked through the hole and looked up at Mandie. "He isn't moving. Maybe he's hurt or something."

"I'd like to get my hands on whoever put him in there!" Mandie said emphatically. "I don't understand what's going on. Ever since we left the ship crazy things have been happening that don't make any sense at all." Her voice echoed back from the damp walls. "Oh, goodness! I'd better be quiet!" she whispered.

"Mandie, I don't see any way for us to get Jonathan out of that room without help," Celia said. "How could anyone ever open that metal door without the key?"

"Celia, where there's a will, there's a way. We just have to figure out the way," Mandie told her, looking about the empty hallway.

"Mandie, what about that carriage we saw come out of the building?" Celia reminded her. "We don't know which way it came. It could have come out of one of those side tunnels."

"I haven't forgotten about that carriage," Mandie assured her. "But it was not the same one we followed out here. It wasn't pulled by Clydesdale horses."

"You're right," Celia acknowledged.

Mandie stooped to look at the bottom of the door. "I don't see any way we could pry open the door from the bottom. But then the lock is so big we probably couldn't get it loose, anyway." She stooped to peek through the keyhole again. Jonathan had not moved. "Jonathan! Jonathan!" she called.

He still didn't move.

"We sure could use some help," Celia remarked. "But we don't even have a way to get back to town and get any."

Mandie walked around in circles in front of the locked door, as she tried to think of some solution.

"Mandie, Snowball is having a fit to get down. Could we just tie his leash onto something so he can walk around a little?" Celia asked. Snowball wiggled furiously in Celia's arms.

"Of course," Mandie agreed. She took her kitten from Celia and set him down while she held onto his red leash. "Let's see, Snowball, I'll just tie this somewhere." She looked around and decided to tie the leash to the handle of the door next to Jonathan's. "There! Now you can stretch your legs."

Mandie turned back to the room Jonathan was in, and the girls tried shaking the door again. It fit so tightly that it wouldn't even rattle. They kept peeking through the keyhole to see whether Jonathan had moved.

"Celia, do you think we could stick something in that hole that would turn the lock?" Mandie asked. "It's so big I can almost reach my finger inside the place where the bolts slide shut." She poked her forefinger into the small open space in the lock.

"Maybe we could force a stick into it and push the bolt back," Celia suggested.

"Good idea!" Mandie agreed.

But everywhere they turned there was nothing but cobwebs.

Celia shivered. "I have the idea this place is never used, Mandie. Look at all the cobwebs," she said.

"Yeah," Mandie said, looking down at the passageway floor. "I can't even see any wheel tracks in the dust on these cobblestones. Just footprints going both ways." Following her Cherokee instinct, she stooped to examine them. "Several sizes of shoes made these prints," she said. "And they all lead to the room where Jonathan is." She stood up and sighed. "Oh, if only Uncle Ned were here, he'd know what to do!"

Uncle Ned was her father's old Cherokee friend. He had always watched over Mandie and often rescued her in times of trouble. But Mandie had not allowed him to accompany her on this journey to Europe.

"I didn't want him to come with us on this trip," Mandie muttered. "You know, Celia, sometimes I sure make big mistakes. I thought I was all grown up because I'd had my thirteenth birthday. I thought I didn't need Uncle Ned to watch over me, but now I realize how wrong I was. I think if I live to be a hundred, I'll always *need* Uncle Ned."

"But he's so old already he couldn't possibly be living when you get to be a hundred," Celia reasoned.

"I don't want to think about that," Mandie said, whirling around to face the door again. She stooped to look through the keyhole. Jonathan had not moved. And she was becoming worried about him.

Suddenly Snowball lurched for a creature that ran across the passageway. The leash stopped him short and the door jerked open.

"That was a rat, Mandie!" Celia squeaked. She held her long skirts high and shrank back against the other wall.

"I know, but it's gone now. I saw it go on down the tunnel," Mandie said, shivering at the thought of such a thing.

Snowball's leash had tangled around him when the door came open, and Mandie stooped to straighten it. When she stood again, she glanced into the cell and noticed another door inside.

"Celia, look!" she exclaimed. "There's a door here that must open into the room where Jonathan is! Look!"

In the dim light from the tiny window high overhead, they approached the dirty door. A heavy metal crossbar held it shut. Snowball, still attached to his leash, followed Mandie into the room.

"Let's see if we can move that bar," Mandie said, glancing around for another place to anchor her kitten's leash. She pulled the outer door to the cell shut and looped the red leash over the door handle.

Pushing up their long sleeves, the girls stood together and pushed up on the bar with all their might. It wouldn't budge. They tried again with no result.

"This door hasn't been opened in a long, long time," Mandie said. "If we could just shake it loose a little, we might be able to lift it off." She gritted her teeth as they pushed upward on the bar again with all their strength.

Suddenly moving away from the crossbar, Mandie whispered, "I hear someone coming. Quick! Stoop down over here." She and Celia squatted in a dark corner while Snowball remained tied to the door.

The voices came closer, from the direction in which the girls had been headed. Footsteps echoed through the tunnel, now approaching the outside door.

"He's in here," said a man with an unusual accent.

The girls held their breath, listening as the door to Jonathan's cell was unlocked and thrown open.

"What's wrong with him?" came another man's voice with a British accent.

"He's just sleeping off the knock on the head we had to give him," the deeper voice replied. "He refused to cooperate and got noisy—"

Mandie was so angry she could hardly keep quiet.

"Wake up, Jonathan Guyer, wake up," the man called.

The girls heard some stirring in the next room, and finally a thick moan. "Let me out of here." It was Jonathan's voice all right.

"We'll let you out just as soon as your father receives our message and gives us what we want," the British voice answered.

"Exactly what is it you want?" Jonathan asked groggily.

"Shall we tell him?" the first voice asked.

"Might as well. He's not going anywhere," the British-man replied.

The deep voice began explaining. "Our job is to gather information for our country," he said. "And we know that your father owns a gun factory here in France. We want all the guns in that factory for our men."

"If your country wants guns, why don't you buy them instead of kidnapping me?" Jonathan asked.

"Because we are going to overthrow our king, that's why," the deep voice replied angrily. "And we do not have money to buy guns. Therefore, your father is going to give them to us."

"I wouldn't be so sure of that. My father never gives away anything," Jonathan told them. "How did you know who I am, anyway?"

"Because of the articles in the newspapers," he replied. "We discovered you were not kidnapped after all, but had just run away from home. That gave us the idea that we could actually kidnap you and get what we want. Smart, heh?" He sounded confident.

"No. Not smart, but awfully dumb," Jonathan answered. "But you are not French. Where is your country? Who are you?"

The British voice spoke up. "That we do not tell."

"It is a long way from here, anyway," the first voice added.

"Have you been in touch with my father?" Jonathan asked.

"No, but we leave here, send a message to New York," the deep voice said.

"You will be freed as soon as we are able to contact

your father and he agrees to our terms," the British voice
assured him.

"We must go now. We have three of your friends waiting," the first man said.

Mandie gasped. Had they captured her grandmother
and the senator? But the man said three. Who would the
third one be?

"Three of my friends?" Jonathan questioned. "What
do you mean by that?"

"Three lovely dark-haired young ladies," the man with
the British accent said.

Mandie grasped Celia's hand. Were those three
strange girls who had been following them around really
friends of Jonathan's? Mandie wondered.

"You are mistaken," came Jonathan's reply. "Those
girls are not my friends. I don't even know them, really."

"But you will remember they made friends with you,
beginning at the hotel in London," the British voice said.
"That was part of our plan. They were tutored to find out
for certain who you were and to get other information
from you by being friendly."

"Do you mean that's why they've been showing up
everywhere I go?" Jonathan asked.

"We are training them to be spies for our country, like
we are," the deep voice replied.

"You two men are from the same country?" Jonathan
asked.

"Yes, we are now," the British accent said. "At one
time I was a British citizen, but I rejected that for a better
country."

"You certainly didn't *reject* your British accent, mister," Jonathan said, sarcastically. "You're still British,
whether you like it or not."

"I won't take issue with your remark now, but I won't forget it," the British voice said angrily.

"We must go now," the deeper voice said. "Remember, we must make another stop at the other end of the tunnel before we join the ladies."

"Yes, they can wait for us," the British voice added.

Mandie quickly figured out their plan. They had come from the other end of the tunnel and would continue on their way in the direction from which she and Celia had come. That would take a while.

Evidently, the three dark-haired girls were waiting at the end of the tunnel from which the men had come. If she and Celia hurried, they could reach the girls before the men returned. She'd like to question those young ladies.

Mandie and Celia heard the men slam the metal door and lock it, then hurriedly walk off.

"Whew! They're gone!" Celia whispered, expelling her breath.

"We still can't get Jonathan out," Mandie said softly. "Let's slip out the other way and find those girls. We can come back here. Like that man said, Jonathan is not going anywhere."

Without alerting Jonathan to their presence, Mandie grabbed Snowball and the girls silently left the empty cell. Lifting their skirts, they hurried down the passageway. Soon they could see daylight and realized they were finally coming to the end of the tunnel.

Mandie stopped and put her hand on Celia's arm. "Slow down. We don't want anyone to see us until we look things over," she said.

"Right." Celia stopped to catch her breath.

Slowly emerging into the daylight, the girls looked

around. They seemed to be in a forest. There was no sign of anyone around except for one carriage—hitched to Clydesdale horses!

The girls cautiously slipped outside and stayed close to the building they had left, keeping shrubs between them and the carriage. As they circled the vehicle from a distance, they spotted the three dark-haired sisters sitting on a low wall out of view of the carriage.

"Let's go!" Mandie brazenly walked out of the shrubs into plain view of the three girls.

The three girls immediately stood up as Mandie and Celia approached.

Mandie stopped in front of the girls and braced herself. "I want to know just who you are and what you are doing to our friend Jonathan," she demanded sternly. "We know he's locked up inside that dungeon room in the tunnel, so you might as well explain what's going on. We're tired of y'all following us, and now you're really making trouble."

Celia took Snowball from Mandie and nervously stood beside her.

The girls gazed at Mandie with a surprised look.

The youngest girl finally spoke. "What are you talking about?" she asked. "Jonathan—locked up in a dungeon room? We didn't do it if he is."

"Oh, but the men who came here with you did, and they said you were the ones who spied on Jonathan," Mandie argued.

The oldest girl spoke. "Our name is Covington. I'm Mary. Maude here is next and Martha there is the youngest. Who are you?"

Mandie eyed them warily. "My name is Amanda Shaw—Mandie for short—and my friend's name is Celia

Hamilton," she said. "But we want to know what's going on? Who are the men you came here with?"

"The man we came here with is our father. The other man is his friend. We don't know his name."

"Your father?" Mandie was incredulous.

Martha, the youngest, quickly corrected her sister. "Well, not really. You see, we're orphans, and a while back, that man and his wife adopted us."

"Where is the woman who is always with you?" Mandie asked.

"Oh, our adoptive mother," Mary replied. "She's waiting in the carriage there."

Mandie's heart did a flip-flop. She hadn't reckoned on running into that rude woman again. And the man had said nothing about the woman waiting for him. She and Celia certainly wanted to avoid a confrontation with her. They didn't need more trouble.

The sisters whispered among themselves, and then Martha spoke. "We did not agree to have Jonathan locked up in a room," she said. "Would you show us where he is? Maybe we can get him out."

Mandie and Celia exchanged glances. It would be risky going back inside the tunnel with the two men expected to come out any minute. But maybe these girls were serious. With their help, maybe they would be able to get the crossbar off that connecting door.

"We'll have to take a chance," Mandie whispered to Celia.

Celia showed the fear she felt.

"If they start anything in the tunnel, we can take care of them," Mandie assured her quietly. "They're sissy city girls, and we're *country* girls. We know how to handle their kind."

Celia finally nodded her assent.

"All right, come on," Mandie told the girls. "This way. But if you try anything, you'll be sorry."

"*Try* anything?" Mary asked. "What does that mean?"

"Oh, it's a good old American expression. 'Don't do anything unusual—just behave yourselves,' " Mandie replied. She took Snowball from Celia and led the way, staying as far from the carriage as possible.

At the tunnel entrance, Mandie told the Covington girls to walk ahead of Celia and her. She didn't trust them behind her.

The girls shrugged and did as Mandie asked.

Mandie held her breath, listening for any sound that might indicate that the two men were coming back. She didn't want to run in to them. They could be dangerous.

If the three sisters could help free Jonathan, Mandie and Celia would find some way back to the city, Mandie was sure of it. But then Mandie remembered the conversation between the men and Jonathan. Neither man was French. What were they doing in this palace? Did the French guards know the men had locked up Jonathan in this place—in Marie Antoinette's great palace?

Where *was* everybody? Mandie wondered. The forest where they had found the girls had been deserted. And they had not met anyone else in the tunnel. She had to admit to herself that those men had her frightened, as well as the fact that there was no one else around.

Chapter 10 / Confrontation With the Spies

The girls soon reached the locked cell where Jonathan was being held prisoner. Mandie leaned over and peeked through the keyhole.

"Jonathan!" she called softly. "It's Mandie and Celia!"

"Mandie!" Jonathan replied at once.

As Mandie watched, Jonathan moved over to the door and looked through the keyhole at her. "Mandie! How did you and Celia find me?" he asked.

"That's a long story, Jonathan. We'll tell you later," Mandie whispered. "Right now those three girls that have been following us around everywhere are going to help us get you out."

"No, no, no!" Jonathan protested from behind the door. "Don't trust those girls. They were in on the kidnapping scheme. Don't trust them."

"But they promised to help get you out of there. They claim they didn't know you were locked up," Mandie told him through the keyhole.

Mary quickly pushed Mandie aside. "Jonathan, please believe us when we say we didn't know what those people were up to," she said. "We *will* help get you out."

"You'd better not be lying to me," Jonathan replied cautiously.

"All right." Mandie took charge again and peeked through the keyhole at Jonathan. "In the next cell, there's a connecting door to your room, but it has a heavy cross-bar blocking it. Celia and I couldn't move it, so these girls are going to help. Maybe together we can get the door open. We've got to hurry."

"Yes," Maude agreed. "Our father will be back soon with his friend."

Without wasting more time and words, Mandie quickly showed the three girls the door. Hooking Snow-ball's leash to the other cell door, Mandie explained what she wanted them to do.

"No problem," Mary said. "Five of us can surely lift that silly old crossbar."

Together they beat and banged and pushed and pulled at the iron bar. But it wouldn't budge. They tried different angles without any luck. Mandie worried about all the noise they were making, but there was no other way to get Jonathan out.

As she stopped to take a breath, Mandie said, "I suppose you're the ones who have been sending mysterious messages and notes."

"Not us," Maude said. "Our mother has been doing that. She also sent flowers to the hotel."

"We *were* the ones who put that note in your journal and then came and took it back," Martha admitted. "We didn't know exactly what was going on, and we didn't want you to get in any trouble."

"Well, that was nice of you," Mandie said sarcastically. "Why couldn't you have come and told us what was going on?"

Jonathan called from inside the room. "Please hurry up and get the door open. Please. Those men will be back."

"You're right," Mandie answered, turning back to the old crossbar.

Suddenly there was the sound of heavy footsteps coming down the passageway.

The girls looked at each other in alarm. Mandie quickly grabbed Snowball and held him in her arms to keep him quiet. Then she softly pushed the cell door shut. All five girls backed off in a corner.

The footsteps stopped outside Jonathan's door, and the deep voice said, "We will be sending you food soon. We will be back."

"All right," Jonathan replied through the closed door.

As the sound of footsteps died away, the girls breathed a sigh of relief.

"Quick! We've got to get that bar off," Mandie said. She opened the cell door and swiftly tied Snowball's leash to it. "They'll go to the carriage, find y'all gone and come back looking for you!" she told the girls.

Spurred on by fright, the girls pushed with all their might and the crossbar slowly became dislodged from its rusty hitches. The iron bar was also rusty, which had created the tighter fit. They still struggled to free the bar completely from the narrow openings on each end.

Mandie stomped her foot. "It's enough to make me lose my temper!" she cried.

"Me, too," Celia agreed.

"Don't give up," Mary said. "We can do it. We've got it loose. All we have to do is heave upward together and force the bar out. Let's do it."

The five girls tried again.

"I wish I were out there to help," Jonathan said through the door.

"Then we wouldn't have to do this!" Mandie replied.

The five girls worked on the bar again. They were making so much noise that they didn't hear the approaching footsteps. Suddenly the bar came free, and they almost lost their balance.

Just then, there was a loud voice behind them. "Just what are you girls doing?" the Britishman asked, snatching Maude with one hand and Martha with the other.

The deep-voiced man grabbed Mary and lunged at Mandie and Celia, but they were too quick for him. Mandie picked up Snowball, and she and Celia dashed out into the hallway.

"Look out!" Mandie cried to Celia.

Celia ran straight into the Covington girls' "mother." As the woman grabbed Celia, Mandie raised her long skirts and aimed a sharp-toed shoe at the woman's shin. The woman gasped in pain, and Celia got away.

Mandie and Celia ran and ran into one side passageway after another as they zigzagged away from the spies. Finally, they had to slow down to catch their breath.

"Whew!" Mandie gasped as she and Celia sat down on the cobblestone passageway. They looked around in the dim light.

"I have no idea where we are now," Mandie said between breaths.

"Me either," Celia said, panting beside her friend.

Snowball clung to his mistress.

Mandie stroked her kitten reassuringly. "Celia, I don't know if we'll ever find our way back outdoors." She sighed. "We need to find one of those guards and tell him what's going on."

"Right," Celia agreed. As she brushed back her thick auburn curls, she felt around for the combs in her hair. They weren't there. Her long hair hung around her shoulders, and her bonnet was clinging by a string. Putting her bonnet back on, she retied it.

Mandie laughed. "You look just great. I'm sure I do, too." She felt for the combs in her hair and could only find one. "Celia, I've lost my bonnet!"

Celia reached behind her friend. "No, here's your bonnet, Mandie. It was hanging down your back," she said, pulling it around.

Laughing again, Mandie tightened the strings under her chin and let the bonnet hang down her back. "Celia, we've got to help Jonathan," she said. "I imagine that man and woman are going to be awfully angry with those girls. They saw us all pulling that crossbar off the door."

"What do you suggest doing?" Celia asked.

"If we can only find our way out of this place and get to a guard, we'll be able to get help," Mandie said. "You know, I can't figure out why there was no one in that part of the tunnel except those spies."

"But since it's an ancient dungeon, no one would know it's being used," Celia replied.

"I guess you're right, Celia," Mandie admitted. "Do you remember the windows high up in the cells? Well, if we could find those windows from the outside of the building, we'd be able to tell where Jonathan is."

"Right!" Celia brightened. "Let's try."

Hastily weaving in and out the corridors, they finally saw light at the end of a passageway.

"Come on!" Mandie cried happily. Holding Snowball tightly, she raced toward the daylight.

"I'm coming," Celia replied, trying to keep up with her friend.

When they finally reached the daylight, they discovered they were back at the entrance where they had come in. There were lots of people around, and there was a uniformed man at the entrance.

Mandie ran up to the man and began talking to him. "Mister, there's someone locked up in the dungeon in that tunnel down there, and he needs help. Please get the police and help us get him out," Mandie babbled.

The man stared at her in surprise. Obviously not understanding English, he began talking rapidly in French. Mandie and Celia tried gestures, but that didn't work either. The man still couldn't understand.

Mandie turned to Celia. "We are a sight to be seen— all dirty and falling apart. He probably thinks we're crazy or something!"

"That's what I was thinking, Mandie," Celia replied.

"Let's try someone else," Mandie said.

The girls began walking around the grounds of the palace, trying to make people understand what they were saying. Some were polite and smiled. Some looked at them in disgust. Some just turned and walked away.

"You know, Celia, I've been thinking," Mandie told her friend as they paused by a water fountain. "We probably should go back and see if Jonathan is still there. Those people might have taken him away because they know we found him."

"Is it possible to find our way back to that dungeon?" Celia asked, doubtfully.

Mandie ran her fingers through the spray of water from the fountain. "I think we ought to at least try," she replied.

As they re-entered the tunnel at the same place they had gone in before, a carriage came rushing out, almost running them over.

Mandie and Celia jumped aside just in time.

"It wasn't the Clydesdale horses," Mandie noted.

"No, it wasn't the same carriage," Celia agreed.

The girls tried to remember exactly the way they had gone before. It seemed to take forever, but they eventually found the dungeon.

"We're on the right path," Mandie whispered, leading the way.

As they finally located the door to the cell where Jonathan had been, they paused and listened. The sound of several voices echoed off the walls. Mandie peeked through the keyhole and was startled to find not only Jonathan but the three Covington girls all locked in the small room.

Silently, Mandie and Celia looked inside the connecting room and saw that the crossbar was back in place. Going back to the keyhole, Mandie whispered loudly, "Jonathan, we're back!"

Jonathan came to look through the hole from his side of the door. "Mandie, please be careful," he quietly warned. "Those people are dangerous. They've even locked up their daughters in here because they were trying to help me escape."

"We've tried to get help, but no one understands English," Mandie told him. "They all look at us as though we were demented."

"Mandie, I have an idea," Jonathan whispered. "Can you learn to say this? *Aidez-moi, s'il vous plaît?* That's "Please help me" in French. Can you say it? *Aidez-moi, s'il vous plaît.*"

"AY-day MWA, seel voo PLAY," Mandie repeated awkwardly.

"That's good enough," Jonathan said. "If you can find

someone and say that to them and then show by gestures that they are to follow you, maybe they'll understand."

Mary moved in front of the keyhole. "The French do not know we are in here," she told Mandie. "This part of the palace is not in use. You will have to show them the way."

"What are those awful people going to do with you girls?" Mandie asked.

"We do not know, but they are terribly angry with us," Mary replied. "I think you should hurry before they come back."

Jonathan came to the keyhole again. "Mandie, don't forget. *Aidez-moi, s'il vous plaît.*"

"AY-day MWA, seel voo PLAY," Mandie repeated again. "We'll hurry. I can't promise anything, Jonathan, but we'll try everything we can think of."

Mandie and Celia hurried off in search of someone to try the newly acquired French on. They crisscrossed tunnels, anxiously looking for anybody except the spies. And they suddenly found themselves at the end of the tunnel where they had found the three sisters earlier. They were in the forest again.

"Oh, goodness!" Mandie moaned. She flopped down on the low wall where the girls had been sitting. "I am tired, and it seems as though all we do is go round and round in circles. Let's rest a few minutes and think this thing out." She let Snowball down on his leash and rested her head on her hands.

Celia closed her eyes and leaned against a statue behind them.

They were silently contemplating the situation when suddenly a low bird whistle jerked Mandie to her feet.

She gasped. "It can't be!" she cried, clasping her hands for joy. "It can't be!"

Celia looked at her friend. "Mandie, what is it?"

There was another low bird whistle.

"Celia, it has to be Uncle Ned!" she exclaimed. "It has to be! That's his signal to me, remember?" Mandie turned 'round and 'round, straining to see through the bushes and trees. "Uncle Ned, where are you?" she called.

At that moment the old Cherokee Indian came walking out from behind a clump of tall trees. He was carrying his bow and arrows and was dressed in the deerskin jacket he always wore back home in North Carolina.

Mandie ran to meet him, and his old face smiled into a thousand wrinkles. He stooped to embrace her. Mandie threw her arms around the old man's neck, and tears of joy rained down her face. She was so happy she couldn't speak.

Celia picked up Snowball and came over to greet the old Indian. Uncle Ned smiled at her over Mandie's blonde head. "Papoose need Ned. Me come. Help." He reached to include Celia in his arms.

Mandie excitedly asked, "Uncle Ned, how did you *get* here? All the way to Europe. I know I told you I didn't need you now that I'm thirteen years old, but I was so wrong, Uncle Ned. I'll always need you."

Uncle Ned smiled. "Ned watch over Papoose like he promise her father, Jim Shaw, when he go to happy hunting ground. Ned watch till *he* go to happy hunting ground."

"But how did you *get* here?" Mandie asked again, stepping back to dry her tears.

The old Cherokee smiled. "Mother of Papoose say Ned must go on other ship to Europe. Watch Papoose. Not let Papoose see."

"I should have known my mother would do that,"

Mandie said with a laugh. "Oh, Uncle Ned, we need your help so badly. Our friend is in desperate trouble."

The girls quickly related the events of the day.

The old Indian listened. "Ned see papooses leave hotel after grandmother leave. Me follow, but lose trail sometimes," he explained.

"Can you figure out what to do, Uncle Ned?" Mandie asked eagerly. "I know you can. You always solve things for me."

The old Indian looked at her and smiled.

Chapter 11 / Unexpected Help

With Uncle Ned's help the girls found the outside window to the cell where Jonathan and the three sisters were imprisoned.

The old Indian examined the bars guarding the opening and shook his head. "Bars not move," he said. "Find other way."

Mandie and Celia led him through the maze of tunnels until they finally found the locked room. Since their last visit there, someone had locked the adjoining room. The girls couldn't show the old Indian the bar across the connecting door.

While Celia held Snowball, Mandie spoke through the keyhole. "Jonathan, we haven't found a way to get you out yet," she whispered, "but Uncle Ned, my dear old Cherokee friend, is here. He can solve anything, and I'm sure he'll figure out what to do."

"Please get us out, too," the oldest girl called.

Jonathan came over to the keyhole. "Mandie, how can you have a *Cherokee* friend in France?" he asked.

"He's not from France. He's from back home in North Carolina," Mandie explained. "He was my father's dearest friend."

"And he came all the way to France? A Cherokee Indian?" Jonathan asked in disbelief.

"That's what I said, Jonathan. Now do you want him to help you get out or not?" Mandie asked, exasperated. "Every minute counts."

"Of course, Mandie. I'm sorry," Jonathan apologized. "It's just so unusual for a Cherokee Indian to come to France."

"And I'm sorry if I sounded sharp, Jonathan. I really didn't mean to. I'm all upset," Mandie told him. "But we've got to get you out, and Uncle Ned can help."

"Those people who adopted us are coming back in a little while," Maude called to them. "I don't want to see them again, so please help us, too."

"I'll do whatever I can," Mandie promised. "If we're able to get Jonathan out, of course you'll be freed, too."

Snowball twisted and turned in Celia's arms, fighting to get down.

"Mandie," Celia complained, "Snowball is trying to scratch me."

Mandie quickly took the kitten and let him down on his leash. "I'm sorry, Celia. I guess he's just worn out," she said.

But Snowball pounced playfully on Uncle Ned's moccasins. The old Indian smiled and rubbed the kitten's white fur. Snowball purred and cuddled against Uncle Ned's hand.

"Why, Snowball, you just wanted to say hello to Uncle Ned." Mandie laughed. "But that's enough for now. We've got some thinking and planning to do." She looked at Uncle Ned, waiting for his suggestions.

"Man and woman come back," he began, barely above a whisper. "I hide. Shoot bow and arrow—"

"Uncle Ned!" Mandie interrupted. "We can't shoot them!"

"Not shoot. Shoot at," the old man said, smiling. "They afraid of Cherokee. Man and woman open door. Ned shoot arrow over heads, not hit. Surprise. Papoose and friends run quick. Get away."

Mandie smiled back at the old man. "I knew you would figure something out," she said. Turning back to the keyhole, she swiftly related their plans. "Uncle Ned will hide and so will we. When those people return and open the door, Uncle Ned will shoot an arrow over their heads, and all of us will have to take off running before they recover from the surprise."

"That sounds like an excellent idea, Mandie," Jonathan told her.

"I hope it works," Martha called softly.

Celia frowned. "What if you should accidentally hit one of them, Uncle Ned?" she asked.

"Uncle Ned never misses his target. Never!" Mandie told her friend.

"But, Uncle Ned, what if those people really hurt one of us?" Celia asked nervously. "You will stop them some way, won't you?"

"Yes." Uncle Ned nodded. "People hurt papooses, Ned hurt people," he told her.

Mary told Mandie that the people who adopted them would probably leave the carriage where Mandie and Celia had seen it before and come into the tunnel from that direction.

Uncle Ned and the girls searched the passageway and found a cross tunnel near the locked room where they could watch for the people to return.

There were cells all along the corridor, and Uncle Ned picked a room nearest the intersection of the two passageways.

"Papooses, wait here," he told them, motioning for them to go inside.

Mandie picked up Snowball, and she and Celia did as he asked. This cell had several small openings in the wall, so the girls could see out into the corridor. Uncle Ned stationed himself right inside the doorway and kept watch.

"When did you actually get to France, Uncle Ned?" Mandie asked the old man as they waited.

"Sun come up this morning," the old Indian replied.

"Then you weren't here when those people took us from the hotel and kept us in that house overnight," Mandie whispered back. "We'll have to tell you all about that awful experience." Turning to Celia, she said, "I wonder if that strange woman from the ship is connected with these girls. Let's remember to ask them."

"They didn't mention her," Celia whispered. "And they didn't say anything about our being with her at that house."

"Papooses quiet. Ears listen for bad people," Uncle Ned cautioned, keeping his gaze on the corridor.

"I'm sorry," Mandie whispered her apology.

"Me, too," Celia added softly.

The time passed slowly. The girls grew tired of standing and finally sat down on the dirty floor. Snowball romped through the room, enjoying his freedom. Uncle Ned remained at the doorway and watched and waited.

No one heard the people coming until they were almost at the intersection of the two passageways. Uncle Ned stiffened. He stared down the corridor. Mandie quietly picked up Snowball, and peeked through a hole in the wall just as the girls' adoptive parents came into view. The man with the deep voice wasn't with them. They were arguing loudly. The woman talked rapidly in some foreign language. The man shook his head vigorously, speaking sharply to her.

As the strangers passed the intersection and disappeared from Mandie's sight, Uncle Ned slowly eased out of the room. He crept to the corner to watch them.

Mandie and Celia crept silently behind him.

Then the crucial moment came. The man took a huge key from his pocket and inserted it in the lock on Jonathan's cell. As he pushed the door open, Uncle Ned sent an arrow in their direction. It whizzed only a fraction of an inch above their heads.

The woman gasped. "What on earth was that?" She turned and saw the quivering arrow imbedded in the wood over the door.

At the same moment, Jonathan and the Covington girls shoved the man out of the way and burst out into the corridor.

Another arrow sailed over the woman's head.

"Indians!" she shrieked.

The man was off balance, but the woman managed to grab Jonathan by his hair as he ran past.

Jonathan howled.

Mandie rushed to the rescue, instinctively flinging Snowball at the woman. He landed on the bodice of the woman's dress, and clung in fright to the lacey frills. The woman released Jonathan's hair.

He and the three sisters followed Celia down the side corridor, while Mandie quickly snatched Snowball from the stunned woman's dress and chased after her friends. They all ducked into a cell down the corridor and waited for Uncle Ned.

The old Indian remained at the intersection of the

corridors with his bow drawn. The man and woman rushed back down the corridor the way they had come. Uncle Ned made sure the man and woman were gone, and then he joined Mandie and her friends.

The dark-haired girls trembled at the sight of him. "A real Indian!" they squealed, backing away as he walked into the room.

"Yes, a real Cherokee Indian, all the way from the United States," Mandie said proudly. "And if it weren't for him, you'd still be locked up—or worse."

Mary stepped forward and reluctantly offered her dainty white hand. "Thank you, sir," she said.

Uncle Ned nodded and ignored the proffered hand. "Welcome," he replied.

"Yes, sir," Jonathan said emphatically, "we all must say thank you. I am so grateful to you."

Uncle Ned nodded and said, "We go now."

With Uncle Ned leading the way, the group finally found their way out of the tunnel and up to the courtyard where people were still milling around. Almost all the spectators turned to stare at Uncle Ned, but it didn't seem to bother him at all. He kept right on walking until he found a guard. Then he turned to Jonathan and the girls.

"Speak French?" he asked the group.

"Yes, sir, I do," Jonathan volunteered. "What shall I say?"

"Police find woman, man," Uncle Ned told him. "French man find way take Papoose and friends to town."

Mandie smiled gratefully. Uncle Ned was going to look after them until they were safe.

The girls and the old Indian watched as Jonathan approached the guard and in French quickly explained the situation they were in.

The guard looked shocked and kept interjecting exclamations in French. Then he bowed to the girls and Uncle Ned and quickly walked into the palace.

"He has gone to find the captain of the guard," Jonathan explained. "They will begin a search immediately for the couple, and also for the other man. And they will take us back to town."

"Does that include us?" Martha asked.

"Why yes, of course," Jonathan assured her.

Mandie looked at the three girls with concern. "But where will y'all go?" she asked. "If y'all go back to the hotel, your adoptive parents may find you there, and there's no telling what may happen next."

"We have a great-uncle—a *real* great-uncle—who will take us in," Maude told her. "He lives in Paris. If we go to the police, they will take us there."

"And we will be so glad to be rid of those people who adopted us," Martha remarked.

The guard returned and spoke to Jonathan, who then turned to the others and translated: "The search has begun, and a carriage will be here immediately to take us back to the city."

As he spoke, an official-looking carriage with a uniformed driver pulled up and stopped before them. The driver jumped down and opened the door. He bowed to the young girls and after helping them inside, he turned to Uncle Ned. The old Indian smiled and shrugged off the driver's offered hand, and spryly stepped into the carriage. The driver returned to his seat and set the vehicle in motion.

"Jonathan," Mandie said as they traveled along, "please tell us what happened that night at the hotel when you didn't come back."

"To make a long story short, two men grabbed me from behind and pushed me out a side door door into a carriage they had waiting in the alley," Jonathan explained. "It was these girls' father and that other dark-complected man, who was from ... who knows what country! I couldn't identify his language."

"Please," Mary objected. "He's not our father. He's just the man who adopted us."

"Sorry. I thought the man was your father at the time," Jonathan apologized. "They took me to a store building near the Eiffel Tower and kept me there until they decided to move me to the dungeon at the palace," he continued. "The traffic was congested around the Tower, and they had to make several stops. I managed to escape from the carriage, but they very quickly caught up with me and forced me back inside."

"Mandie and I saw them do that!" Celia spoke up. "We were right down the street."

"You were?" Jonathan asked.

"Yes, we'll tell you our story later. We want to hear yours," Mandie insisted.

"There isn't much to tell except that they moved me to the dungeon, and said they were demanding guns from my father's factory. You know all that," he said.

Uncle Ned rode along in silence, listening as the young people discussed their adventures.

"What country was that other man from, Mary?" Mandie asked.

"We don't know anything about him," Mary replied. "He was supposed to be a friend of the people who adopted us. That's all we know."

"The police will probably find him and the people who adopted you," Jonathan told the three sisters.

Mandie thought for a minute. "I wonder if they really sent a message to your father, Jonathan," she asked. "Do you think they did?"

"I have no idea, Jonathan replied. "I'll send my father a message, myself, when we get back to the city."

"Uncle Ned, will you be staying at the hotel with us?" Mandie asked. "Does my grandmother know you are in France?"

"No, Papoose, grandmother not know." Uncle Ned smiled. "Not know yet if stay in Paris."

"Grandmother!" Mandie shrieked. "Celia! My grandmother! She doesn't even know where we are. Oh, she is going to be angry with us this time!"

"But, Mandie, your grandmother went off with the senator for the day. They may not even be back yet," Celia reminded her.

"But her friend, Mrs. Lafayette, was supposed to pick us up at the hotel, remember? We were supposed to spend the day with her and her daughters. I wonder what happened when she came after us and we weren't there!" Mandie moaned.

"We may be packing to go home when your grandmother finds out what we've done today," Celia said gloomily.

"I sure hope not," Mandie replied.

Chapter 12 / Final Resolution

When Mandie and Celia arrived at their hotel, they learned that Mrs. Taft had not yet returned. This only delayed their confrontation. Mandie wished it were all over. Her grandmother was going to be awfully angry with her and Celia.

Uncle Ned waited in the lobby while the young people went to their various rooms to bathe and change clothes. After they had joined him in the dining room and begun their meal, the police arrived to question the girls. Mandie had brought Snowball with her in order to feed him, and she tied his leash to the table leg.

Mandie was glad it was Monsieur La Motte who came.

The French policeman put the young people at ease at once. "The palace guards told us the basic details, but please tell me everything you can remember," Monsieur La Motte said kindly. "You first please." He indicated Jonathan.

Jonathan could only repeat what he had told Mandie and Celia. And after those two related their adventures, the Covington girls gave the policemen all the information they could think of concerning the people who had adopted them.

By that time another policeman joined them, informing Monsieur La Motte that the man and woman had been captured and the officers were still looking for the other man.

"For your own safety we must ask you young ladies to stay here in the hotel until we have found him," Monsieur La Motte told the Covington girls. "We will assign an officer to guard you. Do you understand? You are not to go anywhere outside the hotel."

"*Oui*, monsieur," Mary replied. "But we must let our great-uncle know. He will welcome us into his house, we are certain."

"The address please? We will notify him," Monsieur La Motte assured them.

Mary gave him the address.

Maude stifled a yawn. "May we go to our suite now, Monsieur La Motte?" she asked. "We are so tired."

"*Oui*, mademoiselle," Monsieur La Motte agreed. "Monsieur Dubois here will station himself outside your door and see that no one disturbs you. But please remember that you are not to leave the hotel until further notice."

"*Oui*, Monsieur La Motte," Maude agreed. She and her sisters nodded as they rose to leave the table.

Mandie had come to like the girls after all. Her heart ached for them as she thought about the way their adoptive parents had treated them. Maybe their great-uncle would make a good home for them.

"We'll probably see y'all before we go our different ways," Mandie told the girls. "I'm not sure what my grandmother will decide to do when she comes back and hears our story . . . but . . . anyway, I hope that y'all will be happy with your great-uncle."

"Thanks," the three girls replied together.

"And I add my good wishes to that," Celia told them.

"And mine," Jonathan added. "At first I was really angry for all the trouble you caused me. But I can forgive you now. You didn't really know what was going on. And I thank you all for helping to rescue me. You were very brave."

The girls smiled and Martha blushed as they left the table. Monsieur Dubois escorted them out of the dining room.

Uncle Ned had sat silently listening to all the details the young people related concerning the spies. Now he spoke to Mandie. "I leave soon—when grandmother come back," he said. "Papoose not need me. Law man take care of Papoose."

"Oh, Uncle Ned, can't you stay with us for the rest of our visit here in Europe? Please," Mandie pleaded.

The old Indian shook his head. "Business. Must take care of business," he said. "May see Papoose after that."

Monsieur La Motte finished writing his notes and rose. "I must go now," he said, bidding everyone goodbye. "I will be in touch with your grandmother," he told Mandie, "and with the Honorable Senator Morton."

"Thank you, Monsieur La Motte," Mandie replied, smiling. Then she ventured to pronounce another French word, "*Merci*."

"Ah, mademoiselle is learning. *Merci*," he said and left the room.

Jonathan grinned. "That's great, Mandie! You've learned how to say thank you in French."

"I really am going to learn French as soon as I go back to school in September," Mandie said. "I love these people and this country, and I want to be able to talk to them."

"Me, too," Celia added. "But it's going to be awfully hard to learn to speak French—the way they nasalize their words."

Mandie looked at Uncle Ned then back at Celia and Jonathan. "Y'all ought to learn to speak Cherokee," she said. "Now *that's* some complicated language!"

Uncle Ned winked at her. "*Oui*, mademoiselle," he said.

Everyone stared at him in surprise.

"Uncle Ned! Do you speak French?" Mandie asked excitedly.

"No, Papoose," he replied. "Just listen. Copy."

Jonathan laughed. "That's the easiest way to learn a language," he told them.

"My grandmother speaks French, Uncle Ned," Mandie told him. "And speaking of my grandmother, here she comes with Senator Morton," she whispered quickly to the others at the table.

Mrs. Taft and the senator appeared in the dining room doorway, and Uncle Ned quickly stood up.

Mrs. Taft's eyes widened in disbelief. She hurried to the table and sat down. "Uncle Ned! What are you doing here? I mean, I'm surprised to see you—all the way across the ocean like this," she said in astonishment.

The senator took the chair next to Mrs. Taft's and nodded to the old Indian, whom he had met in Washington, D.C.

Uncle Ned smiled. "Papoose need me," he said. "I go now." Turning to Mandie, he added, "See Papoose soon." He patted her blonde head.

"You don't have to leave because we came in," Mrs. Taft assured him.

"Business to do," the old Indian told her. "Soon." He

waved back at Mandie as he left the dining room.

"And what are you girls doing back so early?" Mrs. Taft asked. "And, Jonathan! Where on earth have you been? We have been so worried." She looked flustered, apparently trying to understand how so many changes had occurred since she had left that morning.

"Grandmother," Mandie began nervously. "Uncle Ned helped us rescue Jonathan. Celia and I have talked it over, and we are ready to accept any punishment you may have in mind, but we did finally find Jonathan and rescue him. You see, he was kidnapped."

"What?" Mrs. Taft stared at her in shock.

"You don't say," the senator said with concern.

Mandie, Celia, and Jonathan related their adventures, and Mrs. Taft and the senator sat speechless as they heard what had transpired while they were away visiting their friends.

Mrs. Taft's face showed a mixture of emotions. "Amanda! I will truly be glad when you grow up," she said in frustration. "I suppose I'm just unable to handle one as young as you. This makes me feel awfully old."

Mandie reached for her grandmother's hand. "Grandmother, please don't say that. You're not old. My goodness, you act younger than my mother does and she's your daughter. I'm sorry if I've made you feel bad. Please forgive me."

"It's such a complicated situation that I really and truly don't know what to say or do about it, Amanda," Mrs. Taft admitted. "You and Celia were supposed to wait for Mrs. Lafayette and her daughters to pick y'all up, and then y'all go running off on a dangerous lark in a strange country. Goodness knows what could have happened!" Then she muttered to herself, "I can't imagine why Mrs. Lafayette didn't call me when she didn't find you here."

Mandie bit her lower lip and dropped her gaze. She really felt badly about causing her grandmother trouble.

The waiter brought a pot of fresh coffee to the table and poured some for Mrs. Taft and the senator. Then he left.

Senator Morton leaned forward in his chair and spoke to Mrs. Taft. "I know this doesn't concern me directly," he admitted, "but may I say something?" When she nodded, he continued. "I think that, although there could have been dangerous repercussions, Mandie and Celia have done a brave and worthwhile thing, foiling those spies like that. Why, a war could have broken out somewhere because of what those people were planning."

"I realize that, Senator," Mrs. Taft agreed. "It's just that I'm so upset about what *could* have happened to the girls."

"And there is still one man who has not been caught, Senator Morton," Jonathan reminded him.

"That's right," the senator replied. "But I expect the French police will apprehend him soon. They have an excellent police force who work closely with their national security agents. I'm sure they have brought them in on this matter."

"Oh, what shall I do?" Mrs. Taft muttered to herself.

Just then a nicely dressed man entered the dining room with the waiter, who pointed to their table and left.

The stranger walked straight over to the girls. "Excuse me, mademoiselle," he said to Mandie. "Are you Mademoiselle Amanda Shaw?"

Mandie looked up in astonishment. "Yes, I am," she said. "Why?"

The man offered her a sealed envelope and said, "May I await your decision?"

Mandie took the envelope and turned it over with a sigh. "Another mysterious message probably," she said. "I thought we were through with all that." She hastily ripped open the envelope and pulled out a handwritten note.

She read aloud, "Mademoiselle Amanda Shaw, May I have the honor of your presence at tea this afternoon at four o'clock? Please bring all your friends, including the Cherokee Indian. Signed, Émile Loubet, President of France, the Elysée Palace." Mandie's heart pounded with excitement. She quickly looked at her grandmother.

Mrs. Taft spoke calmly, "You must answer that we will all be honored to be the President's guests, Amanda."

Mandie looked back up at the man who stood waiting. "Please tell the President that we will all be there. We feel honored. Thank you," she said.

The man smiled and said, "*Merci.*" Then he left the room.

"Evidently the President has heard of what happened today," Senator Morton said. "I knew this spy business would draw national attention."

Mandie was excited about the invitation, but at the same time she was concerned. She knew her grandmother would forget about the whole incident of the day because of the President's attention. Mrs. Taft loved social opportunities. But Mandie wished they would have worked things out between themselves.

Suddenly she thought of something. "The President invited Uncle Ned, too," she said, "and he's gone. I don't know when I'll see him again."

"He said he would come back, dear," Mrs. Taft reminded her.

With everything reasonably settled, Mrs. Taft insisted

that everyone get some rest before departing that afternoon for the President's Palace.

Mandie and Celia went to their room and laid down on their beds for a few minutes, but they were too excited to rest. They looked through all their beautiful new clothes and finally decided that Mandie would wear her blue silk and Celia her green one. They were completely dressed long before time to depart.

"You know, Celia, I'm going to have to take Snowball. I'm afraid to leave him alone here," Mandie told her friend as they paraded before the mirrors in their bedroom.

Celia flipped up the lacy ruffle around the neckline of her dress. "The President probably won't mind . . . if you explain why you brought him and how special Snowball is," she replied.

Mandie laughed suddenly. "I'm doing pretty well, getting to meet two presidents in one year. I wonder if President Loubet will be as nice as President McKinley is." She shook out a fold in her skirt.

"Of course we're both partial to President McKinley, since he is our very own president. But the French men are all so polite," Celia replied.

Snowball sat in the middle of the big bed, washing his white fur and pausing to look at his mistress now and then.

Mandie leaned over and patted his head. "That's right, Snowball. You'd better wash yourself real well because you're going with us to see the President of France."

The kitten meowed loudly and went back to washing himself. Then he followed the girls into the parlor.

"You know, I'm anxious to go on to Italy," Mandie told her friend. "I understand they have something there called the catacombs, which is an underground burial place."

"I know," Celia replied. "And they're real old."

"I'd like to go under the ground and see what they look like," Mandie said.

"But not by ourselves," Celia objected.

"Of course not," Mandie assured her. "Grandmother and the senator will be with us, and maybe Jonathan, unless his aunt and uncle get back to Paris before we leave."

"Or his father suddenly comes for him."

"Those spies never got to send their message to Mr. Guyer, so he doesn't know anything about what happened. The police checked it out," Mandie said.

Just then Mrs. Taft came into the parlor in a creme-colored silk dress with lace and accents. She wore a matching hat in the latest French style, and the sweet aroma of French perfume filled the air around her. "Ready, girls?" she asked.

Mandie stooped to fasten Snowball's leash. "Yes, Grandmother," she said.

"Amanda, are you planning on taking that cat with you?" Mrs. Taft asked.

"Please let me, Grandmother," Mandie begged. "So much has been happening. I'm afraid he'll get out of our room somehow and I'll lose him for good."

"All right, but you'll have to apologize to the President for bringing him," Mrs. Taft told her.

"I won't mind," Mandie said, picking up the white kitten. "Thanks, Grandmother!"

When Mandie, Celia, Mrs. Taft, Senator Morton, and Jonathan arrived at the palace and were ushered into the President's reception room, they were surprised to find the Covington girls there.

"He sent us an invitation also," Mary told them in a whisper.

Then the messenger who had brought Mandie the invitation led Mandie and her friends to the President's parlor.

President Loubet was a handsome, friendly gentleman, and he made his guests feel at home right away. Mandie apologized for bringing Snowball, but when she explained, the President said he understood completely. He even reached to pat Snowball as Mandie tied his leash to a nearby doorknob.

"I am so honored to have you Americans come to tea," the President said as they were all seated. "I want to say that my country is very appreciative of the fine work the young people did in rounding up those spies. Our country does not want such people within our borders, and we apologize for any hardships you people may have suffered while guests here in Paris."

"Thank you, President Loubet," Mandie said. "We are also glad to hear that the man and woman who threatened us have been taken into custody. We know the Covington girls are relieved."

The dark-haired girls nodded, and the President smiled at Mandie.

They were halfway through tea when one of President Loubet's guards suddenly entered the room and spoke to the President. "I beg your pardon for the intrusion, Monsieur le President, but there is an Indian outside who insists he must see you. He has another man with him who refused to give his name," the guard said, bowing.

"The Indian has to be Uncle Ned," Mandie muttered to her friends.

"Thank you," President Loubet said to the guard.

"Will you please show the men in?"

In a moment the guard returned with Uncle Ned and the other man the police were looking for. The spy's hands were tied behind his back, and Uncle Ned was using an arrow to prod him into the room.

The President stood.

"French want this man," Uncle Ned said, pushing the man in front of the President.

"You must be the Indian who helped rescue young Jonathan here," President Loubet acknowledged, extending his hand. "Welcome. Please sit down." He motioned to the guard. "Guard, take this spy here and lock him up."

Mandie and her friends breathed a sigh of relief. The other spy had been caught. And of all people, Uncle Ned had brought him in.

"So that was the 'business' you had to attend to, Uncle Ned," Mandie teased with a smile.

"Could not go, leave man loose to harm Papoose," the old man said. "Now Papoose safe."

"Can't you stay?" Mandie begged. "Even for a little while?"

Uncle Ned shrugged his shoulders. "We see," he said.

When they had all finished tea, they got ready to leave.

On her way out with her sisters, Mary came over and spoke to Mandie. "Thanks to your Indian friend we'll be able to leave the hotel and go to our great-uncle's house now," she said. "There's a carriage waiting out front for us."

"I hope to see you again someday," Mandie told the three girls.

Mrs. Taft led the others out the door right behind the Covington girls.

Suddenly Mandie remembered something she had forgotten to ask. Hurrying ahead of her companions, she caught up with Mary Covington just as the dark-haired girl was about to climb aboard the carriage. "Mary," Mandie said, "Mary, please tell me. Are y'all connected in any way with a strange woman who came to Europe on our ship? She has followed us everywhere and caused us all kinds of trouble."

Mary paused. "A strange woman?" she asked. "What did she look like?"

"She's old, gray-haired, and has sharp black eyes," Mandie answered. "She always wears black, flashy diamond rings and a diamond brooch. She's shorter than I am and kind of scrawny."

Mary looked puzzled. "I can't think of anyone I know who looks like that," she replied. "Anyway, I'm sure the police have caught everyone who was involved in the spy business. Good luck." She stepped inside the waiting carriage.

Mandie waved as they drove off and then turned to Celia and Jonathan. "Well," she said with a sigh, "we still don't know who that woman was who held us in that house."

"We may never find out," Celia told her.

"I just hope we never see her again," Mandie added.

After the young people entered the carriage that was to take them back to the hotel, Senator Morton helped Mrs. Taft inside, then climbed in and sat next to Jonathan. "Sorry, Jonathan, I forgot to tell you," he said. "I checked with the newspaper again today, and your aunt and uncle still are not back in the country."

The boy's eyes lit up. "Then I am allowed to go on into Italy with you people?" he asked.

"We promised your father we would keep you with us until your relatives come home," the senator said.

"So I *do* get to stay with you!" Jonathan smiled.

"Right," Mandie answered. "And we want you to show us Italy."

But even as Mandie's thoughts turned to Italy, she wondered about the strange woman from the ship. Would she turn up in Italy, too?